# ATTRACTION

# IN

# ACTION:

## Your How to Guide to...

## Relationships,

## Money,

## Work

## And Health

ISBN: 978-1-60743-898-4

2nd printing version 2vl

Karen Luniw International titles are available at special quantity discounts for bulk purchases for sales promotions, premiums, fundraising and educational use. Special versions or book excerpts can also be created to fit specific needs.

For more information, please write: Karen Luniw International, 2475 Dobbin Road, #22, Suite 714, West Kelowna, BC V4T 2E9 and by email at: info@karenluniwinternational.com or call 250 808-5628.

*For the love of my life, Geoff.*

*It is with your love, support and wisdom*

*that make all this (and more) possible.*

# Table of Contents

## ACKNOWLEDGEMENTS

The idea that I would write a book was reignited in a true Law of Attraction moment. For that, I have Linda Rielly of Peak Potentials to thank. In a conversation she and I had about doing an interview with Harv Eker, Linda stated three times (the magic number for me) that everything really took off for Harv when he wrote a book. It was at that moment I looked up to the Universe and literally pointed and said 'gotcha, I hear ya.' The next day I wrote an outline while I was sitting in the car waiting for my husband Geoff and without a word of a lie, only a few hours later, I received a call from a literary agent asking if I had representation! Could there be a clearer signal?! Not likely.

Ali Brown has been a huge role model for me and I have such appreciation for her inspiration, her generosity of ideas and deliberate openness of her trials and tribulations. Ali along with the late Corey Rudl, are icons and real people all at the same time which has given me hope and a standard to emulate.

I would also like to commend and thank Esther and Jerry Hicks for being the latest brave pioneers to speak their truth and teach so many about the Law of Attraction. Without your courage, myself and many others would not be on this path.

Over the recent past, these angels have touched my life in ways that have had on-going impact: Amanda Maynard, Brigitte

Ballantyne, Crysta Kynaston, Lesley Langton, Donna Rougeau, Doug Meade, James Paterson, Kim Duke, Michelle Morand, Nicole Dunn, Norm LeCavalier, Robert Mackwood, Caroline Sweeney and Scott Paton. Thank you!!!

Lastly, huge hugs and kisses to my pookie, Geoff for kicking my butt, believing in me and giving me the space to create. I love you with all my heart. xo♥∞

## Really, What is This All About and Who on Earth is Karen?

That is a perfectly legitimate question! First, the reason you picked up this book in the first place is what it really *is* all about. Yikes! I promise to be clearer as we carry on but it is true. This book is about the Law of Attraction which is exactly what drew you to this book in the first place whether or not you know about the Law of Attraction or not. Don't worry, we'll explain as we go along...

As for who I am, well, I'm a gal who was working her corporate job and needed an outlet for her passion of teaching people about the Law of Attraction. Being a student of internet marketing (another passion) for years, when I learned about podcasting I decided it was time to see what I could do with this.

By that time, I had been studying and teaching the principles of the Law of Attraction to anyone who would listen for about a decade...long before the movie 'The Secret' came out. When I heard 'The Secret' was being released, I decided it was time to put up a podcast on ITunes and see what would happen.

Within a month my podcast, The Law of Attraction Tips had been downloaded over 18,000 times by people all over the world. To say the least, I was absolutely shocked! Six months later, my podcast had been downloaded over 120,000 times and

11

by a year and a half into this venture, I had over ONE MILLION downloads!

People love what I had to say and how I said it and this medium allowed me to leave my corporate job and start out into my own business (and not a moment too soon!).

At the same time, I was writing a weekly Law of Attraction Tips letter that went out by email to a growing list of thousands of subscribers.  This book is a compilation of all the tips letters from the past two years.  I've included the original, largely unedited, email questions (with names changed and italicized) that came in from both podcast listeners and tips letter readers.  I've taken the liberty of fixing the spelling in the emails so it doesn't drive people like me crazy who are 'Correct Spelling Nazis', or rather, Aficionados. ☺  I've also decided to leave the 'feel' of the writing intact, which is quite informal.  I thought it was important for you as a reader to get a sense of who I am, which is also quite informal and laid back and it's a representation of what my tips readers have been drawn to over the past years.  In advance, please forgive any grammatical errors and liberties.

The tips I give are broken out into five main categories; Law of Attraction Basics; Relationships; Money; Work and Health.  These are the areas that I get most questions about and my answers come from a vast background of coaching and counseling people as well as study of psychology, metaphysics, business, alternative health and relationships. The information also comes from my own experiences, too.

Briefly, I'll tell you my story. I married my high school sweetheart and it didn't turn out so well. Not because we didn't love each other but because we were a terrible match in the first place. Even though I got married at 23 and thought I had it all in hand, the truth was I had no real clue about who I was and what I wanted. Oh sure, I had the basics, fall in love, get married, buy a house, have a baby, yada, yada, yada.

Well that all came to a screeching halt one day when I decided that I would never pick my husband as my friend even though I loved him. Weird place to be! He loved me but didn't treat me all that well and despite counseling, separation and getting back together – love couldn't fix the fact that we were NOT two peas in a pod.

That's not the way it was supposed to happen but that did start my journey.

What I didn't understand, were these two things:

- Why was I so successful at some things and not at others?
- Why were some people successful at the things that I wanted to be successful at?

Ever have those thoughts?  So I started out trying to find out everything I could about this subject.  Add to this my penchant for the metaphysical side of things along with a pretty healthy side of skepticism and logic and my journey split off into many different paths.

Oddly enough, my first introduction to the Law of Attraction came from the business realm and a book by Brian Tracy called **Maximum Achievement**.  He spoke about seven Universal Laws and how to use them to increase your ability to live the life you want to live.

Immediately I started teaching these laws to my clients who were on welfare and who were looking for work.  As I taught these laws, the one that stuck out for me the most was the Law of Attraction.  What I found is that it was simple enough and powerful enough to see in action daily.

I was hooked and started searching (these were days before the Internet and Google!) and it was not easy to find anyone talking about the Law of Attraction but I did see it reflected in many of the days motivational speakers and also in books by masters of the past.  Funny thing was that it was rarely called the Law of Attraction.  That bothered me, and so I set out looking for ways to quell the concerns of the skeptics that I knew I would encounter. Truly, I believe that quantum physics holds the key to this puzzle. Many say that quantum physics proves this law in action but so far the actual quantum physicists that promote this are small in number. In fact, quantum researchers in general don't agree amongst themselves as to which quantum theories best describe the quantum goings-on in our Universe. Given their disagreement however, many are delving into how consciousness affects the quantum universe and this is where much promise lies.

What we're left with is our own experiences and as I watch life on a micro and macro level, I see this Law at work in everything I see. Of course, that's not surprising because that is the whole premise of the Law of Attraction...what you focus on, you see more of!

As I teach and coach people and see the magic unfold deliberately in their life and mine, I'm still amazed and that is what this book is about. It is about sharing the tips and techniques I have used with my clients so you can have a place to begin or augment your understanding of how to use the Law of Attraction in everyday life. We can't wait to hear your stories of witnessing your own magic!

As I was doing my own search years ago to learn more about how to use the Law of Attraction in my everyday life – I was hard put to find anything. Now there are a number of books that

I am Focused

give overall tips and techniques but far fewer that give specific ideas for specific challenges.  That's what this book will give you in many cases – specific tips for specific challenges.

I always think it's a little weird when authors give advice on how to use their book but I've often found value in their suggestions, so I'm going to offer up my own.  Recognizing that most everyone has challenges in one or two areas of their life, reading these specific sections along with the LOA Basics may offer up the most value initially.  However, reading about areas that you aren't challenged in can help you to be a better friend, co-worker or boss by increasing your ability to help others with this information.

This book is also just as useful to flip through to a page that sticks out for you as the information you need to attract for that day.

I decided to have a bit of fun with this book since I have self-published it and added '*I AM*' statements on side of all the odd numbered pages.  This is another way to use this book by flipping to a page and reading your '*I AM*' statement for the day.  These are declarations to the Universe (God, The Source, All-That-Is) that are affirming your state of being which is a very powerful attractor.

## *How to Get a Collection of Law of Attraction Tools – FREE!*

I am so eager for you to get all you can from the Law of Attraction that I have included bonus chapters that couldn't be added in time to this printing, links to all the resources I mention throughout the book and other tools to connect with me and with others about this book and the Law of Attraction. To get your free access go to: www.theattractioninactionbook.com.

Finally, at the end of the book are true success stories from my listeners and readers. This is a small but powerful sampling of what people put the Law of Attraction to use for in their lives (and what I get to hear about daily!). Some relate 'coincidences' of everyday life that these extraordinary people have come to understand that they created. Some stories tell of deliberate intentional acts that created extraordinary results. All are perfect examples. My hope is that they'll show you how the Law of Attraction is working in everyone's life – all the time.

To wrap up, this book is all about the Law of Attraction and how you can use it to impact your life powerfully every day. And I, Karen Luniw, am probably much like you in many ways which means whatever I can do – you can do, too. Isn't that FABULOUS!!?

**Wooohoooo!!!**

# WHAT IS THE LAW OF ATTRACTION?

My favorite definition of The Law of Attraction (LOA) is 'like energy attracts like energy'. Plain and simple. However, what this also requires is an understanding that everything you see and don't see is made up of energy.

EVERYTHING! This includes rocks, trees, air, mountains, sofas, cars, people, thoughts, feelings and beliefs. Cultures, events and places have their own energy, too. If you think about it, you'll know that you've witnessed this in your past experiences.

Since everything is energy, what this means is things of like energy will move towards each other. Good or bad.

Here are some familiar statements that also represent the Law of Attraction.

- Birds of a feather flock together
- Two peas in a pod
- Like attracts like
- Where focus goes energy flows
- Your life is the sum of your dominant thoughts.

LOA is at work 100% of the time whether or not you know about it or believe in it.

Your life is a reflection of what you've attracted into it by past thoughts, feelings and beliefs. If your life is great – keep having the same thoughts, feelings and beliefs! That should be easy because we have an estimated 60,000 thoughts a day and repeat 90%+ of them day after day.

If you want to improve areas of your life, you need to shift what you think, feel and believe (and speak). Sometimes all it takes is a slight shift to achieve the results you want. Sometimes it requires a much larger shift. The great news is that you're totally capable of this shift if you want to make it!

Another thing to know about LOA is that it isn't some woo-woo or New Age concept. It is really no more mysterious than Cause and Effect. You think a certain thought or have a certain emotion which causes you to act in a particular way. The mystery, or the difficult part, is getting to understand that there are many things that affect our thoughts and feelings. Many of these thoughts, feelings and beliefs are subconscious that we are not aware of yet and they affect every part of our life, every day. Because of this, the line between cause and effect is not that clear or easy to uncover. This is why it's easy for people to debunk the power of the Law of Attraction because there seems to be no clear, repeatable (therefore scientific) 'one size fits all' approach. There ARE specific steps to take, which I outline in this book and go into more depth in my *Five Step System* but the path one takes will be different for everyone.

Often people who are new to LOA think that it's just about positive thinking.   Positive thinking certainly is part of the equation but I often think that LOA is really positive thinking on steroids.  (And yes, I have tried to come up with a more politically correct statement than 'steroids' and mega-vitamins doesn't quite do it for me. ☺  If you have suggestions, please email me!)  The main difference is that LOA is about deliberate creation which is more about a state of BEING rather than positive THINKING.  When we get to the state of being that we want to be – nothing will stand in our way.  Nothing.  Getting to that state of BEING is what this process, Law of Attraction and the Five Step System is all about.

Another misconception is that opposites attract and I would say 'Welcome to my former life!' LOL.  In any case where it seems that opposites attract all you need to do is dig a little deeper.  There is always and I mean ALWAYS at least one point of attraction and likely a very powerful one.

In the case of relationships, which is when this topic usually comes up, you probably don't have to look far to see that there was also a physical attraction.  It's the physical attraction that would bring two people together and the characteristics of being 'opposite' would also be part of the package.

Lovers might find the thrill of something entirely different appealing but if the physical attraction wears off and the individuals in the relationship don't take on the enthusiasm of those 'opposite' characteristics – my bet is the relationship is on its way to being over.

I mean really, think about it, does anyone purposely go around looking for someone who is not attractive to them and the complete opposite of themselves and think to themselves – wow, I'm in love! Nope – does not happen in the world I live in.

Most often we are always attracted naturally to people we are most like or most want to be like.

This is a brief overview of the Law of Attraction and what it is – truly, I could write a whole book on it alone.

Below are some basic assumptions I've made about the world as it relates to the Law of Attraction:

- There is a Source energy that is intelligent and all powerful
- There is nothing that this Source Energy is not

- You can tap into this energy and use aspects of it to improve any part of your life
- This law is at work 100% of the time
- Luck and coincidence are the result of the Law of Attraction at work
- Law of Attraction is not a New Age phenomenon; it has been in existence since the beginning of time. It's been referred to in most religions.
- There are steps to help anyone use the Law of Attraction for their benefit - different people have identified different steps – it's all pretty much the same with the premise to make it simple and help people succeed.
- Law of Attraction is a simple concept not always easily applied.
- Automatic attraction is when you create something easily without effort – mostly subconscious.
- Active attraction is the conscious use of the steps, tips and ideas to create what one wants.
- What we think, believe and feel become our reality.
- Like energy responds whether we're remembering something in the past, living it now or imagining something for the future.
- Everything we have now in our life is a result of past thoughts, feelings and beliefs.

# WHY DOESN'T THE LAW OF ATTRACTION WORK ALL THE TIME?

I get many emails lamenting how the person has tried and tried but LOA doesn't seem to be working for them.

Sorry to tell you but LOA is at work perfectly even when you think it's not. In fact, it is a wonderful feedback system. The life you have right now is a sum total of your thoughts, feelings and beliefs in the past. In order to change the effect/results/output (your life today) you need to change the cause/actions/input which is your thoughts, feelings and beliefs.

There are a few reasons it might SEEM like LOA is not working and I've listed them here:

- **Focus on 'Lack'** – This took me the longest time to understand. When we are so clear about what we want and we know we are asking for it – **we wonder why it hasn't shown up yet**. That last highlighted sentence is the focus on lack. When we ask 'where is it?', our energy is focused on the fact that 'it' isn't here yet. The Universe is just a photocopier of our thoughts and it copies them. 'It isn't here' produces 'it' not being here.

23

- **Lack of Belief** – People want to believe but if they feel in their gut or even have a subconscious thought that what they want isn't coming because:
  - It's impossible
  - It's not likely
  - I'm not deserving
  - I'm not worthy
  - I feel guilty
  - Who am I to want this?

  If these thoughts, feelings and beliefs are entertained in any capacity, the Universe HAS to respond. Like energy responds to like energy. If it's impossible then the Universe will make it impossible. If I do not deserve then the Universe will create the circumstances that will reflect your belief, and so on.

- **Lack of Energy/Commitment** – There are a whole host of reasons that contribute to this and most lie in the lack of belief or the lack of desire. For instance, one may say they want to lose weight but if they have tried countless times and have not been successful then their lack of belief exists which contributes to their lack of excitement that this goal could be achieved. Also, if the goal to lose weight is not the individual's goal but rather the goal of another concerned loved one, then the lack of commitment will not create effective results.

- **Law of Rhythm** – Too often we give up 'three feet from gold' which only means that we give up too early or upon first defeat (or second or third). The Universal Law of Rhythm states that everything moves in patterns, seasons or cycles. When we are trying to use new techniques or establish new thoughts, often we don't allow for the Law of Rhythm and give up before our 'down' cycle swings up.

- **Law of Polarity** – This is another Universal Law that states that everything has its opposing energy. Up must have a down, right must have a left, black must have a white, one side of a coin must have another side. More often than not, when we are attracting something, what shows up first is the 'flip-side' of what we truly desire. Most people give up on LOA at this point because they think this stuff doesn't work, when in fact, what they truly want is very close. The funny thing is, when the really crappy stuff shows up and you are confident you've been true to the five step process, this is a time to be celebrating because it's proof that what you want is near.

- **Chemicalization** – This state is an off-shoot of the Law of Polarity and Law of Rhythm. It's the actual process of what is described above – 'when really crappy stuff shows up'. There are four distinct stages that one goes through and it is the time when most people believe that LOA is not working.

I am Truth

25

These are the main reasons I see that influence people to believe that LOA is not working for them. The piece to take away from this is that there is always a reason that LOA **SEEMS** to not be working and it has nothing to do with LOA being ineffective.

## COMMON TERMS

**Belief** – is a thought you have repeated over and over until it becomes a belief. Beliefs can be changed. All one needs to do is start thinking a different thought over and over.

**Theeling** – this is a word I have coined which combines thoughts and feelings. I use theeling to indicate a highly charged thought and feeling together which can be negative or positive. A theeling has great power to change how you act and how the Universe reacts.

## THE FIVE STEPS

## STEP ONE - KNOW WHAT YOU DON'T WANT

Yes, this is contrary to what you may have read or heard elsewhere in regards to the Law of Attraction - but I'm standing my ground on this.

The first step of my Five Step System is, "Know what you **DON'T** want - and then forget about it." Now, say the last line with your best Donny Brasco or Godfather impersonation.

I've been using these five steps for a very long time but when I had these cards made up both *Donny Brasco* and *The Godfather* had been on TV recently. In *Donny Brasco* the question was posed 'what does - forget about it mean?' and I loved that there were a number of interpretations for that simple phrase. The one interpretation resonated with me so much because what I heard was 'just let it go' 'let it fall away'. That's key here because that's exactly what I want you to do after you spend a bit of time to really figure out what you **DON'T** want.

Now back to why I'm standing my ground on this being an integral step to the process. I can't tell you how many people I come across on an on-going basis who have really no clue what they want from their life.

27

It's so easy to get caught up in the process and routine of life and suddenly you find yourself in a rut and feeling frustrated. Now this can happen easily enough, we find a job or create a business that we love and suddenly it starts running our life and we forget what we loved about it in the first place. Same thing in relationships, we find someone, fall in love and we become wonderfully entrenched in each other's lives but all of a sudden, we find ourselves doing things that really aren't of ANY interest to us whatsoever.

I know, I've been there on all the fronts of job, business and love.

Parents are notorious for this - they are wonderful parents and do absolutely amazing things all in the name of their kids (which is fabulous). They end up losing themselves and a sense of who they are and all of a sudden the kids are off to carry on their lives – and the parent is left behind wondering what's important *now*.....

So Step One is really a wake-up call or a shake-up for all of us to step back and review life and figure out what is (if anything) draining you at this time.

Once you do that, do this for all the items on your list:

- Stop doing it and make the choice to be okay with that;
- Keep doing it and make the choice to be okay with that;

- Forget about it - let it roll off your back as quick as you can. Sometimes you'll try to beat yourself up about it but forgive yourself. Like I said - forget about it.

The reason others don't like to include this step is because you don't want the Law of Attraction to work against you and bring you more of what you don't want.

I just want you to become conscious of what you've been tolerating, deal with it and then move on to the fun stuff - creating more of what you DO want!!

I am Love

## STEP TWO - KNOW WHAT YOU DO WANT

Okay, this is the fun part!

You've dealt with being honest with yourself and understanding exactly what you don't want. Now it's time to really focus in on what it is that you *do* want.

Again, for some this is really easy. For those that this is easy - they have already gotten clear on the specifics of what types of experiences they want to have

For the rest, the job here is to allow yourself to be okay with wanting what YOU want.

As mentioned in the last step, many people have devoted their lives to helping others live their dreams. Nothing wrong with that - however, you deserve to fulfill your dreams as well.

Many people also live their life by default, hoping for the best but not really expecting it to happen. Many people live life as if they are being dealt a hand and that they have no say in what the outcome will be. As Tony Robbins says, life will pay any price you ask of it. So, getting clear about what you want is a crucial step.

From the emails I get and the people I deal with on a daily basis, the overlying theme is that people don't believe they deserve much better than the circumstances they are living in today. The fact is that we all deserve to live the life that we truly want - ALL OF US!

Some people feel guilty for wanting more - **GET OVER IT!** Give yourself permission to want what you want AND to start down the road to attracting it!

I truly believe that if each of us was working towards the life we truly wanted to live with positive expectation and with the understanding that the universe is abundant - there would be a whole lot less aggression in the world. It's likely that people would be nice to one another and work at helping each other more. Pollyanna-ish? Maybe, but that's the world I would like to live in - how about you?

Some of the criticism about *The Secret* was around it's focus on materialism. Recently, I was interviewed on a Vancouver radio talk show and that question was raised. I have to tell you, it astonishes me when people want to criticize other's desire to have more of what they want in their life - material or otherwise. I have never run across one person, ever, that didn't want better circumstances for themselves and their family. *The Secret* appeals to this desire - I don't see anything wrong with that - do you?

*I am Abundance*

Having worked with the poorest people in society for years, I know that people are more inclined to feel like they have something to offer and give others when they feel their own needs are being met. That's where learning about the Law of Attraction comes in - give yourself the opportunity to look after your needs in order that you can pay it forward to others when the time is right.

Think big! Think bigger than you've ever thought before. Dream the big dream - how exhilarating is that, if even for a moment or two, you allow yourself to imagine that it could happen?

YOU, yes you, are worthy and deserving of all good things - start writing a list today. Focus on that list - feel good about it! Heck, get really excited about it! It's that kind of energy that puts the Law of Attraction in motion.

## STEP THREE - ASK FOR IT

The truth about this step is that you've already done it. In fact, you're doing it right now.

As soon as you have a thought about what you would prefer in life - you're asking - you're sending out that vibration into the Universe for the Law of Attraction to respond to it.

So why aren't the riches of your thoughts manifesting before your eyes? Well, in fact, the riches of your thoughts ARE manifesting before your eyes - sorry to tell you but whatever you have in your life right now is in direct correlation to the thoughts, beliefs, vibrations and energy you're sending out.

You see, for most people, as soon as you have a thought that "Wow, would I like that" - tell me what your next thought is..... C'mon, you know......

For most people, the next thought is usually a negative one, like "I can't afford that" or "Who am I kidding, better aim a little lower" or something to that effect. Now depending on how much emotion is attached to either of the previous thoughts will determine what you end up having. Chances are the negative thought is more powerful emotionally and negates the positive thought. Again, for most people, things end up remaining the same in their lives.

I compare this whole process to being in the Universal Restaurant of Everything (it's a five star restaurant, of course!) and your Server (her name is LOLA – **Law Of L**ovely **A**ttraction) is at your table ready to take your order back to the kitchen (where ANYTHING can be whipped up).
Unfortunately, most of us can't really make up our mind about what we want.  We know we really want the best item on the menu and sometimes we'll even order it but most times, before our Server, LOLA gets back to the kitchen - we've decided that the item is a little rich for our blood and we decide on something more reasonable.  We call LOLA back and we change our order.  Now, before LOLA gets back to the kitchen in this wonderful Universal Restaurant of Everything - you think again that you really do deserve to have what you want and you call the Server back.  And so the story goes, we keep changing our mind (changing our thoughts) and we never let our wonderful Server, LOLA get to the kitchen.  Sound familiar?

When things are not changing in our life - all we need to do is go back to our thought processes and see if they seem similar to the story above.  I'll bet if you start paying attention - this is exactly what you'll notice in your daily thought process.

The best news is that as soon as you start becoming aware of this tendency to keep throwing conflicting thoughts out - you now can make the choice to stand in your decision to ask for what you really want and stand there in that feeling.  Sometimes this

34

takes courage to want and ask for more than you've ever had before. It takes courage to want and ask for more than what you see others having. It takes courage to want and ask for more than what your friends and family have in their life. BUT, you CAN do it.

What's likely to come up are feelings of doubt, worthiness, guilt, etc. This is your chance to work through these feelings that ARE blocking you from the life that you really want and deserve.

Keep asking for what you want! Asking is powerful. My motto is "If you don't ask - you don't get!"

I am Worthy

## STEP FOUR - ALLOW IT!

This may be the toughest step of all to negotiate. AND, this is the step that most of us get stuck in.

Why would that be? I mean, we've been planning, visualizing, waiting, waiting, waiting....

It's in this step that typically our resistance or our impatience kicks in to high gear. Patience really is a virtue and certainly one that I'm short on - how about you? Do you like waiting for ANYTHING? Do you like waiting for your dreams to come true? We live in a fast food, get-it-now and pay-as-you-go society where waiting for anything means your desire is not being satisfied instantaneously. For some reason we've decided that waiting is a nuisance.

It's the same with our dreams, right? We've ticked off on our list all the things we have to do to get to where we want to go but - darn it all - it's not happening in our time frame! How can that be? I've done all the right things! Where is my (you fill in the blank) new boyfriend, new house, new car, new job, yadda, yadda, yadda (did I mention the bisque?).

Can you tell that I'm writing from my own familiarity with this particular subject? hahaha

Now pay attention to that feeling of frustration, that feeling of 'where is it' and now think about how this strong emotion relates to Law of Attraction..... Law of Attraction just reflects back what we're putting out so - if we're putting out 'where is it' - we're going to get back what? Yes, more of 'where is it'. Not nice, huh? Our stuff isn't going to show up because we're asking where it is - what's going to show up is more of 'where is my stuff?'.

So what do you do? Job #1 is to feel good. Yup, that's your main goal. If you're feeling good - you're likely not thinking about where your stuff is which then allows your stuff to show up on it's own time frame. It's time to trust the process and prepare for when your stuff (your new girlfriend, your new opportunity, your new contact) decides to show up. It's time to get into the feeling of what it feels like when that stuff arrives - that's the feeling that magnetizes and attracts the thing you desire to you.

So, what's Job #1? (Hint: go back to the last paragraph and commit it to memory)

At the beginning of this article I mentioned that impatience and resistance stops what we want from getting to us in this step. I've given some tips about impatience - next - I'll continue on with this step and deal with resistance.

I am Gracious

37

## STEP FOUR - ALLOW IT! AGAIN...

I do think it's important to talk more about resistance because it is a major key to what stops us from moving forward. Did I say major key? I meant MAJOR KEY!!! You see, with impatience - we have acted and are expecting what we want to show up. With resistance, often we don't even get started. We don't allow ourselves to even really consider that what we want will actually show up. We often have some kind of knowing feeling that we shouldn't even get our hopes up.

We've been taught not to get our hopes up from almost day one. As children we have such optimism and often believe ANYTHING is possible. Our very well meaning parents don't want to see us hurt and so advise us to not get so excited.

The thing with Law of Attraction is - the more excited you get and the more energy you put out there - the more likely it is that you will find a way and draw that exact thing into your life!

The resistance you feel in your life now is a result of experiences and more often than not it is that voice in the back of your mind that is like our parent's voice saying - 'don't get all worked up for a possible disappointment' or 'let's stay realistic here' or worse yet - the voice is saying 'who do you think you are - you don't really deserve to have that'.

Often that voice in our head has a feeling attached to it as well and, if you pay attention, you can locate that feeling in your body. For me, the feeling of resistance often feels like a knot in my heart area or my tummy area. Sometimes the feeling can be subtle and sometimes it can feel dramatic - it just depends on what I'm having resistance around.

In the past year I have hit many pockets of resistance because I have been pushing my own limits and going beyond where I have ever been before. It's exciting but I have had to get used to recognizing resistance and acknowledging and pushing through it so it doesn't stop me. That's what resistance does - it usually stops us from even allowing ourselves to dream the big dream. I promise you, you don't want to let resistance stop you from being all you can be.

Here are a couple of things I recommend for releasing resistance:

☐ The Sedona Method
☐ Emotional Freedom Technique

Next, I recommend my own method for pumping you up

☐ The Woohooo Method

The Sedona Method is a series of questions you ask yourself that allows you to release negative emotions.

The Emotional Freedom Technique is a technique that you can do yourself that uses a tapping motion on meridian points on the body to release pent up energy.

My Woohooo Method is borrowing from the Sedona Method and with my own use of questions to really elevate your energy.

Find out more about these methods in your free bonus materials at www.theattractioninactionbook.com.

# STEP FIVE - RECEIVE IT AND APPRECIATE IT

Easy, right? Yes, absolutely - this is probably one of the easiest steps yet the most neglected.

Acknowledging that you have actually received what you asked for is soooo important. Why, you ask? Let's go back to the Law of Attraction - what you focus on you get more of, right? So, if you're focusing on getting what you wanted - what do you think you'll get more of?

YES! More of the things you ask for!

You see, you actually start to put this whole cycle into a repeat motion except now you are in a more profound place because you know this stuff works! When you know this stuff works what happens is that your level of belief and expectation start to rise. When your level of belief and expectation start to rise you become more confident that what you are asking for in this moment has a great probability of happening. If you believe this - you will start to act in accordance with the fact that the thing you want is coming. You begin to just KNOW it and that, my friend, is extremely powerful. When you KNOW something (and you've had this feeling before!) it just happens.

Add to this equation the feeling of appreciation and then you've just added the equivalent of several Red Bull's (a highly

41

caffeinated drink) to the mix and powered it up ten-fold. Remember, whenever you add charged emotion to any thought you have - you have increased the speed of that thing manifesting in your life.

All too often, things, people and events show up in our life and we either forget that we asked for it or we attribute it to luck or something else that we had no part in creating. That's just sad. We miss the opportunity to really experience how powerful we are in our lives and we also miss the opportunity to amp up the receiving of more of what we want.

Start paying attention to what's showing up in your life and think back to whether you had a thought about wanting this thing in your life. Start acknowledging how powerful a role you really do have in creating your life and remember to appreciate or give thanks for all the wonderful things, people and events that continue to show up. You'll truly be amazed at how more and more of what you want appears.

Want more information on how to use the Five Steps? I've created the Five Step System to Attract Anything that lays all of this out in an easy to follow workbook.  Go to www.theattractioninactionbook.com for more information.

# THE LAW OF ATTRACTION BASICS

I am Happy

# DELAYED APPRECIATION…DOES IT STILL WORK?

*a question from a listener….*

*Dear Karen,*

*My name is Barry and I have been pursuing and applying the law of attraction in my life for about a year now.  I just recently discovered your podcast and learned so much more to assist me in changing my way of thinking.  Anyway, onto my problem…*

*In one of your podcasts you mentioned that you need to appreciate all that we receive, whether it be good or bad.  My problem is this, I don't usually notice that I have received something until hours after it has passed (sometimes even days after).  Will my appreciation still be accepted if I don't realize what is happening right away?*

*Thanks for any answers,*
*Barry*

———————

Hi Barry, thanks for the question!  For those of you who are new to my podcasts and tips letters, Barry is talking about Step Five, Receive it and Appreciate it, of my Five Step Attraction System.

In Step Five, your job is to actually acknowledge when what you've asked for shows up! Seems easy enough (like all the other steps) but, as Barry mentions, it's really easy to not notice and therefore let our opportunity go by to give thanks.

The fantastic news is that it's never too late to appreciate something...even hours, days or YEARS later. Some even say that we can actually change past events by changing our mind about them therefore changing our present and future. But I'm going off on a tangent!

To Source Energy, everything is happening NOW so whenever you remember to appreciate something Source Energy receives that message and responds by giving you more opportunities to be appreciative.

And yes, that goes for appreciating the lousy things, too. By appreciating, or if you will, blessing, the negative things that happen, we're actually sending out an energetic vibration that will draw the most positive aspects of that negative situation to our attention. In turn, Source Energy will respond to your appreciation and bring you more positive aspects to appreciate.

Now would be a great time to review those negative things that still have an energetic hold on you and appreciate them. Whaddyathink? Doing this could be the key to unblocking your road to success!

# DO I HAVE THE RIGHT TO FEEL GREAT?

Daily, many of us encounter negative events that range from slight disturbances to absolute potential life changing events.

For the most part, we don't let the little things get to us and we stay positive.  Sometimes we find that these events accumulate or we get hit between the eyes with negativity.  We know that if we are consciously using the Law of Attraction that we want to stay in as high, positive vibrational state as possible.  When we're feeling good - we attract more of what we want into our life!  How exciting is that?

But what happens when the objective of negativity is a loved one?  Do we have the right to try to feel great in spite of them?

One of my audience members wrote in with a similar question.....

## SHOULD I PROCEED WITH HAPPY LAND DESIRES?

*Why is there a word called wrong?    According to God there is no wrong...just simply the soul experiencing itself for who it really is or wants to be????    Soooo  if I "think" "wrong" thoughts....perpetrating my financial and relationship woes...am I or is it a part of my souls preplanned experience to "live out"...or shall I circumvent and thwart the "happenings" by chastising the thought for daring to enter my head and proceed with happy land desires????*

*That's a cry for help. I am soooo upset at myself for breaking up with a man i dearly love but yet i know cannot "live" with due to the fact he likes to tell me and or remind me of all I need to do to "correct" myself and that I need "help". He calls himself a positive thinker yet with me he announces all or any little nuance of a "mistake" I seem to create.*

*My financial world is in total collapse with repossessions of two vehicles and a foreclosure on a house and bills to pay with little income.*

*W.*

————————————

Thanks for writing to me with this question!

Unfortunately, this seems to be a case of 'the worse it gets - the worse it gets'. You can't get any more evidence of Law of Attraction then that - when one is on a downward spiral - one tends to attract more fancy bad stuff. It's truly important to understand AS SOON AS POSSIBLE that you deserve far better than what you're experiencing right now.

If we did, in fact, pre-plan our experiences before we got here - I truly am a believer that we always have **free will** and can make choices in the moment that will either lead to us happiness or in the other direction.

It's really crappy when you have to leave others behind when you realize that they aren't as positive as they think they are. If you know my story - you'll remember that I had to do exactly the same thing. I left a man I loved because we weren't a good match - he picked EVERYTHING I did apart. You know, while it was hard for a bit - believe in your future because it is bright, girl! If you know my story - you'll also know that I'm with an absolutely awesome guy who loves EVERYTHING about me. You can have that too (but with a different guy, okay! LOL)

So, you've made the first step in the right direction and you've left the relationship. Perfect!

This is something that I recommend when you're dealing with negative situations. It's not the first step but I expect you've already tried some other options. This is exactly what I talk about in my just released _Seven Secrets to Staying Positive in Negative Situations_ teleseminar audio.

It is so important to take the appropriate measures to protect yourself when you're encountering negativity or low vibes because it can affect all aspects of your life.

48

Next, make sure you find things to do that make you feel good. You see, it works in the opposite direction, too and you've likely experienced it in your life. The better it gets - the better it gets. So you just need to start initiating some fun things or at least some activities that make you feel good. You have the right to feel great - you just need to start choosing that.

Once you start making these choices - you will see your life start swinging in the right direction. Ya, sure there will still be days here and there that hit you where it hurts but get up - brush off and get back at feeling great. Proceed to your happy land of desires!

I am Cheery

## DO THE WOOHOOO!

Since I'm off having fun this week, I thought I'd leave you with the Woohoo Method that I created. It pumps your energy up, boosts your belief and tells the Universe that you are ready receive!!

Ask yourself these questions and answer in the way I provided:

1. Can you imagine what you want to be, do or have in your life? *Yes.*
2. Would you imagine what you want to be, do or have in your life? *Yes.*
3. Are you ready for it? *Yes.*
4. When? *Now.*
5. Does that feel awesome/incredible/fantastic? *Yes!*
6. How awesome/incredible/fantastic? *WOOOOHOOOOOOOOO!!!!*

I recommend doing this out loud and with as much enthusiasm as you can muster. I love to do this in my car.

# YAHOO - SPRING IS HERE!

Okay, well not officially but it is getting warmer - the snow is melting (not fast enough for me!) and I'm hearing more birds sing outside.

My pooches are loving every minute of it since they can be outside more now and are full p*** and vinegar.

Do you notice that people are happier when the sun starts to shine?  Do you notice how that's contagious?  Smiling has the ability to let loose all kinds of good feeling chemicals in our bodies and by doing this we attract more good stuff into our lives just by this one simple act.

Do a great thing today for yourself and someone else and pass a smile on!

I am Discerning

## TROUBLE FINDING A GUITARIST

*Karen,*

*I have a couple of things to say today. Love your show and because of your show I got "The Secret". It was everything you said it was and more. I must say that because of your demeanor and easy way of explaining something that could sound complicated. Thank you for making these concepts so accessible. I imagine this is why your Podcast is catching on. Lots more people feel the same way I do.*

*I have a question for you...*
*As you may remember, I am a songwriter and I have a band. We were a 3 piece. I wrote the songs, sing lead and play bass and my best friend is the drummer and we HAD a guitarist. Well we had to get rid of him because he wasn't right for us.*

*It's been a year without one and I'm slowly dying... Well, not really, I just feel real depressed without my vehicle for my art. So, if you could give me any tips on attracting the perfect guitarist. I've done all I could think of but no success as of yet. I cannot understand why I am having trouble attracting this which is so important to me.*
*Anyway, thanks for all of your hard work.*
*Peace,*


*Charlie*

---

Hey Charlie - thanks for your email. Can you imagine what your music would sound like with the right guitarist? Imagine it being easy to find this person because the right connections are going to put you two together. Watch for it. Anyone could put you two together - anyone at all! Imagine practicing with someone who gets your vibe and gets your music. How great would that be? That's a great question to ask yourself.

Stop focusing on the lack of the guitarist. Stop thinking about why the last one didn't work out. Stop replaying what happened with the last one and why he wasn't right.

How great is your music going to sound with the right mix? How great does it feel when it all gels and the music flows just right? How awesome is it when it all just clicks? That's where you want to be - that's where you want to spend your time, focus and emotion - in these last questions.

Do that and your guitarist is going to show up on your doorstep.

I am Extraordinary

# DO YOU ASK YOURSELF GOOD QUESTIONS?

Years ago I heard Tony Robbins say something about the power of asking yourself great questions. It can be totally transformational. It completely fits in with the Law of Attraction because if you're asking yourself - *'Why did this happen to me?'* as opposed to *'What can I do so this doesn't happen again?'* - you recognize that you will attract completely different answers.

I've gotten pretty good at asking myself good questions but weirdly enough Brad Pitt has inspired me to think bigger. Find out how below....

## VIVID DREAMS AND A MOVIE STAR

Today I'm veering off my regular path a bit because I had an interesting dream the other night that I want to share with you. I know, does anyone really need to know about my intimate dreams about Brad Pitt. Well, not generally, in fact, I never have dreams with movie stars in them but this one was noteworthy for what it taught me about myself.

So, I had quite a vivid dream about Brad Pitt and he told me that he thought what I was doing with my podcasts and tips letter was great and that he believed in me. (Seems normal enough, hey?

;)) Then he asked me what success in my business would mean to me.

It was quite interesting - not because I hadn't asked that question before of myself but because the question came from someone I felt could help me achieve anything. Again, this is very interesting because I've asked myself this question previously from the perspective that *anything was possible* and also from the perspective that I'm *co-creating with Source Energy*. Because I believe in limitlessness I thought I had the vision pegged. However, now I started to answer this question with a feeling of more possibility because I knew that Brad could help me in ways I hadn't considered before - therefore expanding my definition of success. The question made me think differently.

I woke up completely and utterly surprised - what did this mean? How could this dream and the question from someone I don't know expand my vision? Do I think that Brad Pitt is all-powerful? NO! I think he's doing some great things to help others but all-powerful? Hardly.

What I came up with is that Brad Pitt is tangible. He is a live, tangible person who has means to affect the world positively if he chooses. That's a little easier to grasp than limitlessness and the power of Source Energy.

I am Deserving

So enough rambling, what does this have to do with the Law of Attraction? (I can hear you, you know - LOL)

Well, I bring this forward for a few reasons.

- I want you to expand your vision of yourself and your life by asking yourself great questions. If you do that - you will be far more likely to attract that expanded vision into your life.
- Pick someone who you admire that you feel is powerful and successful and imagine that person asking you some important questions. Would you answer differently if you thought they could help you? If you can imagine this - you are more likely to attract the vision and someone who can help you. Not necessarily the person you had in mind but someone or a number of other people who could help you.
- Finally, I want to warn you to not eat too much turkey, potatoes and gravy - it obviously has mind-altering effects - LOL!! (We celebrated Thanksgiving this past weekend and that's really why this story unfolded.)

# WHAT ABOUT PLAN B?

Ahhh, Plan B, our way out if things don't work. C'mon, admit it, for just about everything you want to have in your life or currently have, you have a plan just in case things don't work out, right?

It's looks something like this....I really would love to have that new Mini Cooper S but that Dodge Caliber has a great payment plan.... I'd really like to go for that great job but I'll apply for this other job that I don't really want..... I really like that guy I met last week but this other guy has been asking me out and he seems nice enough.... I'd like to save the rainforest but I have get my laundry done and it's been a hectic week and what can I do, anyways.... I'd like to make $100,000 this year but I should be grateful that I have any job.....

Do you catch the drift? Plan B is really Plan BUT.... Did you notice that every scenario started with a desire and mid-way we got a but followed by the alternative. Think about it, what do you think you're attracting when you ask the Universe for one thing and immediately follow up with a different request? If you answered, 'nothing changes', you'd be right!

Look, I understand that we've all been programmed to have an alternative plan in things don't work out. It seems prudent, even common sense. The problem is that you're sending out mixed messages and the status quo remains.

*I am Stupendous*

If you want change, real change in your life, you have to send out a strong and consistent message that will be able to attract like energy. You need to identify what it is that you truly want and ask for it. Have faith that if you really do have to come up with an alternative that you will! In the interim keep your focus squarely on what you truly want. You'll attract it much faster!

# WHERE'S YOUR HAPPY PLACE?

Hey, we all have bad days or weeks, right?

I highly recommend finding your happy place that you can go to in your mind. As cliché as it sounds - taking a moment to be there when you're experiencing times of stress can do wonders for you.

Mine is a beach in Cancun where Geoff and I spent the best holiday of my life. It's morning and we're sitting on the beach and the sun is already hot even though it's only 9 in the morning. I can feel a warm breeze on my face and all I can see is sand and the sun shimmering on the blue, blue Caribbean. Ah, heaven.....

Your happy place will be specific to you and it should bring you a sense of peace and/or happiness. Remember it when you're feeling stressed or bummed out and you'll immediately start to change your vibrational level.

I am Woohoooo!

## DO YOU KNOW HOW POWERFUL YOU ARE?

Take some time to think about this concept. Do you know how powerful you are? Do you know you are the creator of your life? Do you know you co-create with a very powerful force?

If you knew that - I mean, really, really, knew that - what would you do differently today? Tomorrow? Next week?

Beside you - whose life would you be changing if you acknowledged how incredible you are?

How are they (and you) missing out by not acknowledging this?

# WORRYING ABOUT 'THE HOW'?

Okay, you know what?  If you do worry about how you're going to manifest or attract what you want - you are trying to do the Universe's (God, Allah, Source Energy) work.  That's not your job!  One of the audience has a question about this below......

### Life of Wealth in London - But How?

*Hi Karen:*

*I am trying to get over the idea that something is too big for me to attract.  I want to attract a life of wealth in London.  First, I need the wealth to get there and buy property.*

*I look up property in London on the Internet, and picture myself there.  I listen to the "London Walks" podcasts and imagine myself walking down those same streets that he is describing and having plenty of money to survive.*

*"The Secret" says that you should just ask and let the Universe worry about the how.  Do I ask for the money or the life.  I want to live in London more than anything.  It is a passion now.  But, I want to live a rich, full life, wealthy in all areas.  I don't want to go there and struggle.*

I am Excited

*Any advice will help.*

———————————

Thanks again to the audience member who wrote in with this question! As always, every question I get represents a similar question that's sitting in the minds of a good portion of my audience - so thanks for being brave and sending this in so others can also receive the answer.

The information you heard or read in 'The Secret' is absolutely correct - don't worry about 'the how'.  There are literally millions (or my favorite word - gazillions!) of ways you could find yourself in London.  There are countless ways this dream can manifest BUT if you try to imagine it happening one or two specific ways - you are directing Source Energy's flow and because it is obedient to the Law of Attraction - it tries to orchestrate that particular scenario.  And, if you're like pretty much the rest of the population on this globe - you probably are changing that scenario and how it can happen daily (if not hourly :)) in your mind.  This sends mixed messages to Source Energy and voila - nothing much changes.  A reminder - YOU are soooo not alone in doing this - this act alone keeps the majority of what all of us want at bay.

My best advice is to do what you have been doing and continue to imagine walking down those streets and picture yourself there. Also, in your imagining this, get into a strong feeling state - how would this feel to be there? what would it smell like? who would be with you? what emotional state would you feel? You really want to get excited about this.

Ask yourself these three questions and then you have to, absolutely have to, say the last statement out loud and with as much enthusiasm as you can muster where ever you are :)

1. Can I imagine this?
2. Am I ready for it?
3. How awesome does this feel?

(This is the statement to say out loud as enthusiastically as you can..) WOOHOOOOOOOOOO!

You see, it is our emotion that really puts the gas in our boat. It is strong emotion that makes things happen. Think about it - the times that you have made big changes in your life were usually motivated by some very charged emotional state. Love, anger, frustration - you name it - these emotions are strong motivators to action. However, it's not just *your* action - your emotions are vibrating out to the Universe and it's reading it and bringing you a match to that vibration. Emotions are really energy (e) in motion = e motion.

You do have the potential to go to London and live their without struggle. You need to rid your mind of that option (struggle) and

*I am Cheerful*

only imagine living there with all you need. Don't waver from this thought and you will create it, you will attract it! How awesome would that be?!

Let go of your thoughts (or rules) about how this all has to happen. Do you really need to buy property there to be there? We know that everyone that lives there doesn't own their own property. You need to ask yourself what's the most important aspect of this goal - living in London? owning property? being wealthy? I'm not saying that you can't attract it all - you really could but I wonder if it's the whole package or some of the items of the package that's bringing up resistance for you. Would receiving one or two aspects of this creation feel easier to attract? Only you can answer that.

I really look forward to hearing about your new life in London! It will happen - just keep your focus.

# DON'T YOU HATE WAITING?

I don't know about you, but I HATE waiting! Hmm, what do you think I'm creating with *that* kind of emotion?

Yet waiting is often an absolute necessity in the creation of what we want. Sometimes the waiting allows us to grow into the person that can actually allow and be congruent with what we are asking for. While we're becoming the person that we need to be, it's very likely that we'll start to have different experiences.

Think back to a time when you really wanted something to occur in your life. I'll bet that between the time that you identified what you wanted and the time that it arrived - all kinds of growth experiences happened. Situations that allowed you to clarify what you wanted and didn't want. Remember Steps One and Two to Attracting What You Want? (I'll have these up on my website very soon if you missed the original emails) Also think back and I'll bet that the endless period of time spent waiting collapsed into nothing when what you wanted finally showed up.

I remember the couple of years between the break up of my marriage and when I met Geoff - the time seemed absolutely, excruciatingly long BUT when we finally met - it's like all the time waiting seemed like nothing. Go figure!

I am Blissful

One of the biggest reasons people reject the Law of Attraction is because what they want isn't showing up. When people start using the Law of Attraction consciously, they get clear about what they want, they ask for it and then after a bit of time has gone by, wonder where the heck 'it' is. This is usually the time where they start to question whether all this stuff really works.

The thing to remember is that the Universe is basically photocopying your thoughts so if you're thinking 'where the heck is it' - you'll have that lack of 'it' showing up reflected back to you. 'Here ma'am, here's your hard copy of your thoughts' - otherwise known as your reality.

So what do you do about it? There are a bunch of things you can do but the first thing to do, always, is move your thoughts from 'where is it' to taking time to live in the moment of having what you want and getting excited about it. Simple...and necessary. The more time you can devote to this simple action - the faster you'll see what you want arrive at your doorstep. Try it out!

# DRAMA - LESSON ONE AND OTHER WHIRLWINDS

I don't know if this story has gone beyond North America - but it's fascinating how, even in death, whirlwinds of energy still spin off some individuals.

Anna Nicole Smith is the person who, even weeks after her surprising death, is consuming some news and entertainment shows. What I know of her life is a blatant display of the Law of Attraction. A display of how the Law of Attraction works in a negative sense.

It seems a good portion of Anna Nicole's life was filled with drama and she attracted people into her life that became part of and perpetuated that drama. (I mean, give me a break! Zsa Zsa Gabor's husband could be the father! Good grief! Next, Elvis will be showing up and saying he's the father!)

Today, weeks after her death, the amazingly sad story continues at an incredible level of intensity and my sense is that the drama will continue - like a legacy. An energetic, vibrational legacy. Wow, who would want that!?

I bring this up because I think it's something we'd all like to avoid in our life (and after-life) however, I think it is an easy,

*I am Laughing*

observable example of the Law of Attraction at work. With Anna Nicole's story - it's pretty easy to see that 'drama vibration' at work; who it's attracted and the results of that vibration. Here's the class list in this Drama class of life: Anna Nicole - leading this drama class; Daniel (the son who died at A.N.'s bedside - 3 DAYS AFTER SHE'S GIVEN BIRTH!); Vergie (the Mom); Howard K. (important that you get that initial in there) Stern - the father listed on the birth certificate that hardly a person (that knows anything about the story) believes is the real father; Larry, The Prince, the old bodyguard and probably countless other men - who all swear they are the father (I, personally, think the baby looks like Larry); the Florida judge (was this guy entertaining and wild, or what?); the best friend (who could only talk about who A.N. was 'doing' and not 'doing'. Oh ya, let's not forget the really old dead billionaire that A.N. married when she was practically a teen-ager. I mean, really, I don't know that the best writers in Hollywood could write a story as drama-filled and bizarre as this real life story.

Who's enrolled for this drama class? The little baby girl, Dannielynn. Let's all send this little one a vibration of love, peace and extreme happiness in her life - she is currently living unaware in a whirlwind of drama - she could use some different energy coming her way, I bet!

I know the topic of Anna Nicole Smith is not for everyone but it is so 'in your face' Law of Attraction - I couldn't help but write about it. It is perfect in its display of its power.

In the whirlwind of your life - what kind of energetic twisters are you sending off? Are they happy ones, sad ones, drama ones, prosperous ones? Something to think about. :)

Remember to get all your free bonus materials and links to resources mentioned throughout this book at www.theattractioninactionbook.com

I am Tickled

# GETTING BACK TO BASICS

Today I thought I would revisit some basics. Many of you listen to my podcasts but I know some of you are just finding them for the first time so some of you will have heard this information from me before. I find when I go back and review information - whether I gravitated to it or not - I am always surprised to see something new that I hadn't seen before.

There are many people out there talking about the Law of Attraction these days and many have slightly differing definitions of the Law of Attraction. The definition I like to use is that like energy attracts like energy. I always follow up that definition with the fact that we are all made up of energy and is everything around us. Whether it's the chair we're sitting on, the air we're breathing or the trees we can see in our backyard - EVERYTHING is made up of energy.

All different forms - whether it's the tree, the chair or your thoughts - vibrate at a certain level. Those things that vibrate in similar or identical frequencies will 'clump' together. They are attracted to each other and therefore will end up together.

It's the same with our thoughts - what we think - we vibrate and therefore attract. Everything that is around you is a result of what you've been vibrating.

This is the statement that usually is a sore point for some people and understandably! If things are crappy in your life right now - do you want some blonde Canadian gal to be telling you that you're creating this? I didn't think so ;) However, stay with me here - if the concept of the Law of Attraction is new to you - keeping an open mind is key to getting the things that you want in your life.

You see, many of us, ah heck - ALL OF US - repeat certain patterns in our life and some of those patterns produce good or great things and some of those patterns create lousy stuff - over and over and over again. Sound familiar?

I'll paraphrase Einstein as he described this phenomenon by stating that the thinking that got us in to this problem will NOT be the same thinking that gets us out of this problem. That's why keeping an open mind is very important because in order to change things in your life - you need to change the way you think.

By changing the way you think, you change the rate at which your thoughts vibrate at, which, in turn, ATTRACTS what you want to you.

So, for those of you who felt a little irked at my statement above, the thing about this is that it is really great news! Whaaaa....?! I know, I can hear it now, Karen, you've gone off your rocker -

I am Thrilled

how can knowing that I've created this mess I'm in be great news?

I thought you'd never ask! hahaha The great thing about this and the great thing about the Law of Attraction is the understanding that the power to changing things lies within us. And, that is fabulous! Sure, external events that are not great are going to continue but now, with the Law of Attraction, you can start to change what you do with those external events and that, my friend, will make all the difference in your life!

You see, we all have the power to have the life we want - we just have to start changing the way we think (and vibrate!).

Isn't that exciting?!

# GETTING BEAT UP BY THE LAW OF ATTRACTION...

**This email comes from a long time friend and client so my answer is embedded in the email in CAPS. And yes, I did let her know that I wasn't yelling because I was writing in capitals. :)

*Hey Karen,*

*I'm not so sure that you would want to use this as one of your shared questions/comments, but I do have something I want to share with you and ask for your feedback.*

ANYTIME!!!!!!!! I'M REALLY GLAD YOU WROTE ME.

*Twice in the past 6 months I have had a very traumatic experience of being really upset about something and having a "friend" first and then my sister second rant at me that it was all my fault because I obviously attracted this situation.*

DON'T YOU WANT TO CRACK THEM OVER THE HEAD!? :) YOU KNOW I BELIEVE THAT WE ATTRACT EVERYTHING IN OUR LIFE BUT THE LAST THING ANYONE NEEDS WHEN THEY'RE FEELING BADLY IS TO BE TOLD 'IT'S YOUR FAULT'. QUITE HONESTLY, IF YOU COULD HAVE, YOU WOULD HAVE DONE THINGS DIFFERENTLY TO CREATE A DIFFERENT OUTCOME.

I am Excellent

73

WE'RE ALL HERE LEARNING TO FIGURE OUT AND GET
PAST OUR 'STUFF'.  SOME THINGS WE'RE BETTER AT -
OTHER THINGS WE NEED TO KEEP WORKING AT.
THAT'S THE KICKER.  ANYWAYS, DO-GOODERS ARE
NOT DOING GOOD WHEN THEY'RE BERATING
SOMEONE FOR WHAT THEY 'SHOULD' HAVE DONE.
HINDSIGHT IS 20/20 (USUALLY!  HAHAHA)

*Most recently it was regarding my breakup with my boyfriend
last week. She went so far as to give the example of how much
better her inspiring friend is dealing with her breakup and using
the Secret to do so.*

THAT'S GREAT FOR HER FRIEND!  SOMETIMES WE
JUST NEED TO MOURN OUR LOSSES AND STAY THERE
FOR A BIT.  WE NEED FRIENDS THAT CAN SUPPORT
THAT UNCOMFORTABLE STUFF. FOR THOSE THAT
CAN'T HANG OUT WITH YOU DURING THAT PERIOD -
DON'T INVOLVE THEM.  YOU'RE BETTER OFF HANGING
ON YOUR OWN DURING THAT TIME RATHER THAN
BEING IN AN ENVIRONMENT THAT MAKES YOU FEEL
WORSE! I HAVE FRIENDS THAT CAN'T HANDLE
EMOTIONAL STUFF - THEY ARE THE LAST PEOPLE I GO
TO WHEN I NEED SUPPORT.  THEY CAN'T HELP - THEY
DON'T KNOW HOW.

*My breakup had just happened and I was still in shock and grieving my loss. In both examples they were using the premise of LOA to kick me when I was down. I am not exaggerating by saying that they were both quite cruel about it. I have decided not to share anything personal with these women and to limit my exposure to them.*

WISE IDEA! I TRULY FEEL OUR REASON FOR BEING IS TO FEEL JOY, FEEL GOOD - IF YOU'RE AROUND PEOPLE THAT CAN'T HELP YOU LIFT YOUR SPIRITS - STAY AWAY FROM THEM - CUZ THEY CAN'T HELP!!

*As you know I have been working with LOA for nearly a decade now. Sometimes, it is easier than others for me to follow. I think it is a good tool for empowering one's life, but I have recently found that some are really using it as a weapon to blame, judge and make others feel inadequate.*

I am Jubilant

YUP, THAT CAN HAPPEN WHEN AN IDEA BECOMES POPULAR - IT CAN BE USED BY THOSE WHO ARE NOT SKILLED IN IT'S DELIVERY DURING THE TOUGH TIMES.

*I am questioning my beliefs about LOA.*

UNDERSTANDABLY!!

*There are some things I feel that I can affect more than others.*

YES, THAT'S TRUE! I HAVE THINGS THAT ARE
ABSOLUTELY SIMPLE FOR ME TO MANIFEST BUT BY
GOD, I STILL HAVE MY OWN ISSUES - SHEESH!!! IT
COMES DOWN TO OUR SELF-TALK AND BELIEFS AND
HOW AWARE WE ARE OF THEM AND HOW OFTEN WE
CONSCIOUSLY MOVE AWAY FROM THOSE THOUGHTS
THAT DON'T WORK FOR US.

*I don't feel that I can (or should) control the actions of others.*

YOU CAN'T CONTROL OTHERS BUT YOU CAN
CONTROL HOW YOU REACT TO THEM.

*I realize that when I am happier then others are kinder to me.*

:) THAT'S PROBABLY FAIRLY UNIVERSAL! REMEMBER,
MEAN PEOPLE SUCK! LOL

*I have also noticed that sometimes I can be positive and focused
on my creating and still have "bad" things happen...such as
breakups, death of loved ones, illness etc. The struggle I am
having is that when these things happen I know it is best to get to*

*feel better ASAP, but there is also a natural grieving process and an acknowledging of feelings.*

EXACTLY!! YOU CAN'T GO FROM FEELING CRAPPY TO FEELING THAT LIFE IS A BOWL OF GIGGLES - DOESN'T WORK THAT WAY. WE REALLY NEED TO GO THROUGH THE PROCESS AND THE FEELING BETTER GENERALLY HAPPENS GRADUALLY. THE MORE WE PRACTICE THE BETTER WE GET AT FINDING WHAT WORKS TO CHANGE OUR STATE TO A MORE POSITIVE ONE AND AT SOME POINT SHIFTING GETS EASY.

*I really do work hard on incorporating these principles into my life. After so long there are still things that I have been unable to make significant changes such as my health, occasional depression, weight, and finances. The part that doesn't work for me is that if I am creating my reality and I still haven't accomplished these things then either I am failing*

NO SUCH THING AS FAILURE!!!
*because I am not positive enough all the time or that there are in fact just some things that one cannot control.*

IT'S NOT ABOUT BEING POSITIVE ENOUGH - IT'S ABOUT CHANGING OUR BELIEFS ABOUT WHAT IS POSSIBLE FOR US AND SHIFTING THE BALANCE OF

I am Delighted

UNDERLYING THOUGHTS/BELIEFS FROM THE
OPPOSITE OF WHAT WE WANT TO MORE OF WHAT WE
WANT. WE CAN'T STICK A HAPPY FACE ON IT WHEN
WE REALLY DON'T FEEL HAPPY OR POSITIVE OR
HOPEFUL. THE UNIVERSE RESPONDS TO HOW WE
FEEL ABOUT SOMETHING NOT HOW WE WOULD LIKE
TO FEEL ABOUT IT. I DON'T KNOW IF ANYONE SAID IT
WOULD BE EASY - IF THEY DID - THEY SHOULD BE
SHOT!! THE COOL THING ABOUT LOA IS THAT THE
CONCEPT IS SIMPLE - THE PRACTICE, FOR SOME
THINGS, CAN BE TRYING AND THE FARTHEST THING
FROM EASY.

*I would really appreciate if you could share some inspiration
with me.*

I HOPE THIS HELPED - THE BEST THING YOU CAN DO
FOR YOURSELF IS TO GO AND DO SOMETHING THAT
MAKES YOU FEEL GOOD. THAT'S ALL IT IS ABOUT.
FORGET ABOUT YOUR GOOFY FRIEND AND SISTER
AND FORGIVE THEM FOR WHAT THEY DON'T KNOW. I
AM CONFIDENT, IN THEIR OWN WEIRD WAY THAT
THEY WERE JUST TRYING TO HELP YOU BECAUSE
THEY LOVE YOU. JUST DON'T GIVE THEM THE
OPPORTUNITY TO SHOW THEIR LOVE THIS WAY
AGAIN! HAHAHA

# GETTING OUT OF YOUR OWN WAY

Recently, I shared a video with you that is now on my blog and the response I got from so many of you was overwhelmingly positive.

The video was part of a competition where students submitted their video with the theme u@50.  This particular video came in second place - man, I wonder what got first place.

In any case, oddly enough, I had a couple of people send me nasty emails saying the video sucked and how dare I post it..... Whaaa?  Really?

The only explanation that I could come up with is that the people didn't watch the video all the way through the WHOLE TWO MINUTES.  In any case, it's proof that despite my urgings to stay with it and watch - they didn't.  How often do we all do this?  We're urged to listen or hang in there and we don't because we can't see from the starting line how it can help.

I'm not pointing fingers, gosh, I almost let myself fall into this same trap myself this past week.  Friends were throwing out some ideas and I was ready to dismiss them because I couldn't see how they would work.

When we get caught up in the 'hows' of anything, we don't let the Universe work its magic.

79

Luckily, I had two separate conversations, one right after the other with two unrelated friends saying virtually the same, exact thing to me.  It wasn't until my second friend was half way through her sentence (and I was literally shaking my head) that I had a sudden wake up call.  I had just heard the same thing not even half an hour before.  What did I do?  I opened myself to the possibilities and I know without a doubt that these ideas will be HUGE in my life.  To think I was ready to dismiss them....

Anything you're dismissing lately?

# GRATITUDE MASTERY AND MANIFESTATION

Ever notice that it's easy to give thanks and appreciation to the Universe AFTER you've gotten exactly what you wanted? Sure, it's pretty easy! What you've wanted has shown up and boy are you glad - all kinds of vibes of gratitude are running rampant. The world is your oyster and you couldn't feel better! Yahoooo!!!

But what about those moments when your brain is giving you grief and you're having a mental argument with yourself about whether or not you're wasting your time actually believing that what you've been focused on is going to show up? You looooove giving thanks and appreciation then, right? NOT!

The truth is that many of us actually do forget to appreciate and give thanks when what we want does show up never mind *before* it shows up. However, this is another one of those really quick ways that you can get your vibration in alignment with what you actually want which, in turn, manifests it for you quicker.

I like to call this Gratitude Mastery - if you can actually give and FEEL thanks and appreciation for what you want BEFORE it shows up, that is a true sign of a master. It means you're putting out a vibration of expectation and WOW is that powerful. You're actually choosing to operate in an alternate universe where what you are asking for already exists.

Can you feel the difference between these two statements?

- I can't wait for world peace
- Thank you, I appreciate world peace now

Which statement is more attractive to sensing and creating world peace? The first statement implies that world peace does not exist. The second statement beckons the speaker to look for and witness world peace now which, in turn, attracts more opportunities to witness world peace.

So, whether it's world peace, money for groceries, a new love interest or new appliances - show the Universe your appreciation first and see what shows up.

# ACTING ON INKLINGS

I often get asked how the Law of Attraction works in my life - where would I even start? Every day is absolutely a fascinating unfolding of the Law of Attraction in action.

Here's what happened today:

- Last week I wrote a list of people I would like to be associated with - on Tuesday I got a phone call from a person I have not yet met who knows, personally, two of the people on my list! Crazy, hey?

- The other day I had been lamenting to myself that I never get to actually meet the people that my tips letters and podcasts have impacted.

Today I met a lady in Prince George who used to live in my home city of Kelowna - she thanked me for impacting her life. She used the tips and techniques in my tips letters and podcasts to get the job she wanted AND to buy a house that closes tomorrow. Incredible - man, I'm living it and it still gives me shivers!! Of note, I had walked passed this gal a few times today and I got an inkling to introduce myself. It's acting upon those inklings and inspirations that make life rich. Who knows, I might not have heard this great story nor had it to tell if I hadn't acted.

83

This was just today!  There's no reason we can't all live in this manner - it's just about becoming more conscious about what we want and then taking inspired action.

# FRIDAY THE 13TH – GOOD OR NOT?

Is this a day you are superstitious about?

Definitely is for me - I have had absolutely wonderful things happen for me on this day.

You see, our thoughts are so powerful that we can choose a specific day and attach a specific meaning to it that can affect t outcome of that day.

What's tomorrow going to be like for you?

*I am Content*

# HAVE WE MADE A MISTAKE USING THE LAW?

*Dear Karen .....*

*I am writing to you from Amman Jordan, and since I have read The Secret book and saw the DVD three times, but until now we (as a family) did not receive any answer from the Universe to our demands, still I have no doubt and have lots of faith, and we encourage each other, every day I go through any sight in my computer that leads to the Secret and read everything that might be helpful, so my question to you, is there a possibility that we have made a mistake in any stage of our law of attraction?*

*Let me tell you that we have done everything, step by step, and in our minds we do believe that we are getting what we have requested, still it is not there yet, I do not want my family to be suspicious. Can you help us and give us more details or direct us to the proper path, to ensure us that we are getting our demands soon.*

*We have asked for a home that we own and a car and a bank account, since we do not have any of them.*

*My best wishes for you.... awaiting for your answer.*
*FG*

---

Thanks for writing!

Sounds like you're suffering from one of the top ten reasons that keep MANY people stuck where they're at! This is a common 'mistake' people make when applying what they have learned about the Law of Attraction.

I call this a **lack mentality** which just means that while you have likely done all the right things - what you're doing **now** is focusing on the **lack** of the house, the car and the bank account. The Universe has answered your demand - your job now is to allow it to happen and quite honestly, this is where most of us get stuck. (So you are in company of a great many people!)

There are many things that you can do to turn this lack mentality around and for today I will share one of the most powerful tools you can use.

Focus on **appreciating** all the things that you have already created. I guarantee that if you look there IS something that appeared today that you hoped would appear. Be thankful for anything and everything.

What this starts to do immediately is put you in the **vibrational state** of 'having' as opposed to 'lacking'. If you are appreciating what you have - you'll access that feeling of abundance in the

87

time called NOW - which is all that counts. The Law of Attraction will respond by giving you more opportunities to feel abundant and grateful - which means that the things that you want are moving closer to you.

# HOW AM I GOING TO GET WHAT I WANT?

Face it, we all really like to feel like we're in control, right!? Of course! And, for those of us 'recovering' control freaks - sometimes this Law of Attraction thing all seems a little bit daunting. Speaking from experience...yada, yada....I really get this.

The problem is, the more we try to control and try to figure out *HOW* our stuff is going to get to us - the more we create resistance to the very thing we want.

The finite (you and me) cannot do the work of the infinite (Source Energy, God, Allah, The Universe...). We can't even begin to fathom the multitude of ways our good can show up for us.

See if this scenario described by one of my audience sounds familiar to you, check it out...

## HOW DO I GET OUT OF MY OWN WAY?

*I have identified exactly what I want, and am visualizing it as mine already, and am feeling grateful for it. I know I'm not supposed to worry or even think about the "how" of it becoming mine. That's the part I'm struggling with.*

*The house that is perfect for my family is on the market.*

*However, I have a major financial obstacle to overcome before I can sell my current home. There is no action that I personally can take right now to overcome that. So I am going ahead with plans to get my house ready for sale. The problem is, I can't let go of this obstacle, and my husband has convinced himself that this dream is already shot down. This is causing me much anxiety which I know is interfering with the vibration I should be feeling.*

*How do I let this go in order to let the universe do its work? I've heard a little about the "shadow" getting in the way of the law of attraction. How do I get out of my own way?*

*Thank you for your help! Your podcast is so uplifting and enjoyable.*

*Frankie*

———————————

Thanks for your email Frankie. This is such a great question and a very common question in it's variety of ways it shows up.

There are two things I would like to address out of this question. First, getting your house ready for sale is a great thing to do! Geoff and I are in the process of doing that now, too. We know pretty much where we would like to move to but haven't a clue when or how it's going to happen. The fact is, that's not our job. As mentioned above, the infinite (Source Energy) has, of course, an infinite number of ways that it can bring you what you want. We can't even begin to figure out what 'behind-the-scenes' orchestrations are happening. I like to think of Source Energy as a movie director who is putting a scene together and can create any circumstance she wants in order to pull off that event in that movie.

You ask what do you need to do to let the universe do it's work and there are a few things I would suggest.

- Let go of whatever that financial obstacle is and you can do that by not giving it any attention or energy. Don't think about it and if you do - just......
- Focus on examples from your life or others when seemingly impossible events all unfolded to create a wanted result.
- Love the house you're in and love the house you want.
- Have faith that the right thing will happen at the right time and the house that you want (or an even better one) is on it's way to you. So even if the other house sells - it just means it wasn't the right match to you. There really is a better one out there for you.....REALLY!!!
- Let go of that particular house having to be 'THE ONE'.

As soon as we start trying to figure out 'HOW' or if we become attached to only one certain outcome - you are creating a wall (resistance) between you and what you want. When we are trying to figure out 'HOW' - we are inadvertently giving attention to the fact that the thing we want isn't there. When we focus on what we want not being there - guess what.....? You got it, there is a lot of energy tied up in lack and is a strong attractor. We end up attracting more of what we're focusing on - the lack of that thing being present. Not at all what we want. Also, when we focus on one specific outcome - we are literally giving energy and instructions to the Universe of how we think it should be done (hmm...sound a little like control?). Law of Attraction works to make that happen - the problem is, we're likely making it harder for it to come about because certain conditions have to all line up. When God is in charge - the path of least resistance is taken and it might not look at all like what we were trying to orchestrate. Therefore, we are likely putting off our good so everything can line up rather than trusting it to All-that-Is.

The second thing out of your question I want to address is the ability to keep your vibration high when you're in the presence of negativity. I'll suggest one thing to start and when you get a chance, listen to my podcast, *Staying Up Around Negative People Preview.*

The one thing I will suggest, since it's your husband, is to ask him what he would like to see happen. What this does is divert the focus immediately on 'the reality' to a higher vibration feeling of 'the way you'd like it'.

Keep focusing on what you want and keep preparing your house for sale - the Universe will pick up on that!

I am Rich

# HOW DO I GET RID OF ENVY?

*Can you please teach me how to use the Law of Attraction for getting rid of envy? I hate this feeling that I have. Someone I love very dearly has recently come into a lot of money and I hate that I envy her.*

*Thank you,*

————————————————

Envy and jealousy are such crappy feelings - aren't they? Thanks for sending me this email - I know it's hard to even admit these feelings to ourselves sometimes.

The goal is to move your vibrational level up a level or two to start. You see, this feeling you're having really isn't about your friend as much as it's about your belief in lack. (Which is a pretty hard belief to squash when it's hittin' you between the eyes daily) So here's a few things you can do to start to switch this feeling around:

- Forgive yourself for feeling this way about your friends good fortune (this will start to raise your vibration) as the feeling comes more from your belief in lack and your lack of belief in abundance (more than enough for all - an unlimited supply)

- Start appreciating all the good things that you have in your life right now
- Start appreciating all the good things about your friend
- Look for evidence of abundance around you and appreciate it
- Ask for more of the things you want and start to create an expectancy that it will happen

Taking action on each and every one of these items listed above will start to move you in the right direction. You'll start to feel better and you'll start to attract more of what you want in your life.

I am Affluent

## ABSENCE OF EVIDENCE...

Some of you may have heard this quote from me before and forgive me if I've referred to it recently but I think it's particularly a useful statement at this time of year.

Absence of evidence is not evidence of absence.

or

God's delays are not God's denials. (Substitute God for Universe or whatever works for you)

Perhaps this is a world-wide phenomenon but certainly in North America - the few months after Christmas can sometimes be slow on the business front. People don't have money, they're peopled-out and/or they're escaping to warmer climates. It's easy as a business person to get discouraged. However, if you look around - there always is someone thriving in this timeframe. Why?

Well, it's usually because they're the person who doesn't let the conditions of life determine their mood and mindset. Their mindset and mood determine the conditions of their life.

These people also know that what they want is coming and that often NOTHING happens before the BIG stuff hits. Have you ever noticed that?

# ASK FOR WHAT YOU WANT, DARN IT!

Always trying to be conscious about what is going on around me - when things start showing up in two's and three's - I know it's time to pay attention.

This has been a week where the focus has definitely been about communication. Or rather, the lack of good communication.

We teach people how to treat us and if we're not getting what we want in our relationships or at work - things start to fall apart for us. You see, if we teach (allow) people to treat us poorly or with disrespect or take advantage of us - we'll just get more of that and then we wait........ and wait.......

We wait for something to change (hopefully that other person! Sheesh! I mean, after all, they ARE the problem!) or someone to come and fix the problem or, more often than not, wait for someone else to commiserate with us about how awful that other person is.... hmmm..... sound familiar?

Well, guess what!? It ain't going to get better. In fact, it's likely to get worse if you don't make some changes. Ok, what does this have to do with the Law of Attraction?

97

I thought you would never ask!! :) Communication is a huge part of the Law of Attraction. How we communicate things to ourselves, to our friends, family and co-workers and to our Source Energy determines what we get back (attract back) in to our lives. Getting clear about our communication is key. You see, it's likely there is some pay-off for you communicating ineffectively - it's up to you to figure out if that pay-off is worth you not having the life you want.

The whole premise of the Law of Attraction is based on 'ask and you shall receive'. All you have to do today is look around and see the result of what you've been asking for as it is a direct reflection of (albeit, not consciously!) this fact.

The question to you is then - is your life a reflection of what you would ask for if you knew you were asking?

If your life isn't reflecting what you truly want - I've got great news for you! You can start changing it today and in no time it will be a reflection of what you want on-going.

# AM I DELUSIONAL TO BELIEVE IN SOMETHING OTHER THAN WHAT I SEE?

*Dear Karen,*

*We've been hit by so many unexpected things lately. My husband has to change jobs because his boss couldn't afford to pay him. we've both had costly motor accidents and we owe heaps of money in unpaid bills. Luckily the wolf has been kept away from the door, but I still freak out. I've been trying to stay calm in all this. I know it's all old stuff coming to hit us. We'll get through it, however my husband is Mr doom and gloom. The more positive I am the more negative he becomes. He said something the other day which I thought was very telling and he has a point, if you feel as though you're a millionaire when there's not a red cent in the bank , then you're delusional. I got really hurt by that and very confused. Any suggestions? I love listening to your pod-casts and reading your weekly blogs. They've been especially helpful especially at this time. I wonder if I'm missing something?*

*We all have our own rules - it's our way of being. Our rules come from our beliefs about the way we think about the world. In turn, we attract into our life things that are in accordance with our beliefs. Makes sense, right?*

I am independent

---

Thank you so much for sending this email in! Would it help if I told you that you're not the only one feeling this way?

You're absolutely right about the fact that we attract into our life things that are in accordance with our beliefs. So, as a result, what's happening now is nothing more than a reflection of what you've been vibrating up to this point. That can change!

Another thing to keep in mind, (that I always find good news to my ears) is that we live in a world of duality or polarity. The Law of Polarity states that you can't have one side without the other. For instance, you can't have good without bad, up without down, right without left, etc.

In this case, you can't have all this lousy stuff without good stuff being really near by. If you've been 'asking' for more, bigger and better - then it's just the negative stuff that's showing up first. Your job is to hang tough through it - keep your focus and energy on what you truly want and YOU WILL get make it to the things that you truly want. The key is not to let 'what is' distract you from what you want to be. This process is also called chemicalization and Catherine Ponder writes about this in her book *Dynamic Laws of Healing* - good info!

Remember, our outer circumstances are not who we are inside. They are a reflection of what we have been thinking, feeling and believing but they don't reflect who we truly are - someone absolutely worthy of all good things!

I am Great

# ARE YOU CHEMICALIZING?

Recently I've received quite a number of emails from people who have been applying the Law of Attraction to their life and suddenly find their life turned upside down. Here's an example of one that I received and a follow up email....

*Date: Tue, 15 Jul 2008 14:50:34 -0700 (PDT)*

*Hi Karen!*

*I appreciated your last newsletter about loving your place to dwell professionally.*

*While I do love my profession as Director of Events, I keep getting sucked in by bad female bosses who are either menopausal crazy, psychotic, egotistical or have their head so far up their you know what, that it hinders my success in getting things done. More than often, the female boss is a key decision-maker when it comes to my event planning process. I feel frustrated and stuck. Please help me find a way to generate good energy and help me move towards a better professional place with no crazy boss. I'm a productive Virgo - I can't stand people who live in lala land.*

*Date: Wed, 06 Aug 2008 12:30:36 -0700 (PDT)*

*The follow up to this email is that I got fired for knowing too much and my boss had an inkling that I would blow the whistle on her.*

*I wanted so much to love it but I just couldn't anymore. Now I have to focus finding a job in the midst of this bad economy. I'm sad!*

---

Thanks so much for your emails - especially the follow up!!

The interesting thing about the Law of Attraction is that when you start identifying what you truly want in your life; starting asking for it and start focusing on it - YOUR LIFE WILL CHANGE! That's the exciting part!

The harder to swallow part is that the change (and the manner in which it occurs) doesn't always happen in the way we might prefer - especially if we're not clear with the Universe about HOW we would like to see the change occur. Let me clarify that last part - it isn't your job to figure out the 'how's' but you CAN ask for it to be easy.

There are a number of things to talk about with this email and what you are attracting but what's most obvious is that your spirit

*I am Rolling in It!*

is asking (loudly!) for a better environment. Now you have the opportunity to get really clear about what you don't want; what you do want so you can ask for it, allow it and have gratitude for it. What you're going through right now is what is called chemicalization which is the 'rough patch' where the Universe is aligning itself AND YOU with what you do want.

You know the saying it's always darkest before the dawn? Well, this is an example of it and your job is to stay focused on what you want and stay positive. In fact, NOW is the time to be thankful for what you're about to receive. If you can be thankful in advance, you are showing such faith in the Universe and this acts to speed up the process of what you truly desire.

So, for starters, this is what you need to do:

1. Get clear and use the Five Steps to Attracting What You Want
2. Stay positive
3. Be thankful in advance for what you're asking for

I really look forward to getting the next follow up email with your progress!

# ARE YOU ON TRACK FOR THE YEAR?

Ahhhh, just a few more months and the year will be behind us. Has it been the year you hoped it would be? Have you accomplished or manifested the things you wanted?

It's a good time to sit back and take stock of where you're at - are you closer to your goals or further away? Do you still want for the same things?

I find that this is a great time of the year to gear up again after a lazy summer (or winter depending what part of the world you're from) - focus your attention, take time to get your inspiration and take action. Inspired action is all we want - anything else is just work for work's sake.

*I am Talented*

# HOW DO I GET BACK ON TRACK WHEN I HAVE NEGATIVE THOUGHTS?

*Hello,*

*Thank you so much for this pod-cast and for bringing us some much great information and help in regards to the laws. I listen to your podcast on ITUNES.*

*My name is Anne, I live in NY-35yrs old, married mother of two terrific kids (4yr old daughter & 2 yr old son).*

*I am a newcomer to this way of thinking and your pod-casts are a great way to help me incorporate the process in my life and daily thought processes.*

*I have some basic questions on using the laws (correctly);*

*I know that the book "The Secret" (page 47) talks about writing down what you want, asking for it and that you only have to ask once-like placing an order in a catalogue.*

*What happens in those times that you feel so frustrated with the circumstances in your life and that you are living" life by default"(I first heard this term on your podcast-episode 3). Like you, I have felt I was more of a 'people-pleaser' and this as of this year I started to ask myself what I want (yes I am also a mother and you make reference that moms go through this a lot - I see it already although I've only been a mom for a short time). Sometimes I find myself reverting to my old thinking which was at times very negative and very much defeated in attitude. When you have those 'relapses' does it put you many paces behind or further away from what you DO want? How do you turn that around and get yourself back on track?*

*Also when you say to make a list of what we would like to do, be or have (and what we don't want) do you mean in the material aspect or anything that we truly want to 'have' i.e. happiness, peace etc?*

*Thank you for answering this email.*

———————————————

Thanks for your question Anne! The fact is we ALL have times when we revert back to 'old thinking' and that's normal. It doesn't matter how much we've learned, how far we've come or how enlightened we become - we all revert! We also all revert back to old patterns of behavior when we are stressed, tired or overwhelmed. Pick any one of those three, and likely you'll find a mom feeling that way :)

The great news is that relapses are okay. They help us to become really clear again about what we don't want and when we're ready, we're even more convicted about where to focus our energy.

Do these relapses move us away from what we do want - yes, but only temporarily and usually in direct proportion to the intensity of the feeling you're having during this relapse. So, if you're only mildly ranting and raving (lol) you haven't moved off the path too far. If you're really ranting and raving - you're just ensuring that you're going to get more of what you DON'T want. **So stop that as soon as you can!** However, when you're done with it and come back to your Law of Attraction senses - your job is to get pumped up, excited, enthusiastic or any positive feeling you can attach to and get to a really good feeling place.

Imagine a teeter-totter with every good feeling you've had about a topic on one side and every lousy feeling you've had piled up on the other side. Imagine that energy accumulating on either side as you have a positive or negative emotion - that's what's happening as you're sending out those vibrations into the Universe. The thing to be aware of is that, for the most part, you probably started on the positive side of the teeter-totter and so any negative feelings don't have a really huge effect.

As far as the actual 'how' of turning it around - appreciation and gratitude are very strong ways to flip your energy. Appreciate and give thanks for ANYTHING and you'll notice a shift if your energy. Read books or anything that inspires you. Listen to inspiring speakers or music. Do anything that feels good and you will start to bump that teeter-totter to the positive side. (Remember getting 'bumped' as a kid on a teeter-totter? What a fun thought!)

As far as your question about making a list of what we want to do, be or have - I mean anything, material or not. In the end, with whatever we want to do, be or have - we want these things because we believe it will help us to feel a certain way whether it's happy, peaceful or any emotion. So writing down the types of feelings you want to have is very useful but so is writing down the tangible and intangible things that you think will help you to feel those feelings.

For instance, as a Mom, you want your children to be happy and healthy and likely that might help you to feel a myriad of feelings which could include happiness and peacefulness - so writing down 'I have happy and healthy children' would be more than appropriate.

That's a great question as to whether this applies to just material things - specifically because there is some criticism floating around 'out there' about Law of Attraction and the movie 'The Secret' being ways to promote greediness and materialism. I know I'm preaching to the converted but it's simply not true.

I am unbelievable

Law of Attraction works for anything and everything, whether it's wanting to buy a car you want, get a parking spot, find the love you want or creating an organization that will help our environment or needy people or groups.  The ways one can consciously use the Law of Attraction is only limited by one's imagination.

# ARE WE HAVING FUN YET?

Amid all the really negative financial news of the past few weeks, I'm wondering if you've taken some time to have some fun?

I'm amazed that even as a Canadian, how wrapped up I've gotten in the news about what's going on in the US financial markets. What has become abundantly clear is that we are all very interconnected and interdependent. What happens to one really does affect all.

What's good about this? (BTW, this is a FANTASTIC question to ask anytime you're facing something really negative)

Well, what's good about this is that we can move from the macro to the micro (or from the all to the small) and imagine that what each of us does individually really does have an impact on others.

SO, take some time to have some fun, feel good and play. Turn off the doom and gloom news for awhile (yes, it will still be there when you decide to turn it back on). By doing this you WILL have an effect on others - guaranteed. In fact, it is your duty (yes, I said duty) to intentionally go out and have some fun this week - imagine the good vibration you'll be spreading out to the world.

*I am Abundant*

## A TRIBUTE TO MY SALLY-BEAN

A couple of weeks before Christmas we had to say so-long to our sweet little Sally. She had been part of our family for 13 years.

Salvadora Dali-mation was what Geoff and I named her when she first picked us but she became Sally-bean to me. 'Bean' because she was a real-live 'being' to us, she certainly seemed more human than pooch from day one. She (and I) was even featured in a Victoria, BC magazine Focus on Women...she's very photogenic! :)

Sally was a vocal and happy gal. She barked like the dickens at visitors and loved to scratch her back after dinner on the lawn. She was also the first one to truly teach me about total self-acceptance. She just expected love (and treats) from everyone just because she was who she was, Sally.

While we all miss her, we understand that this is just a transition in energy and she's off playing at her favorite place, Dallas Road in Victoria. I swear *that* is the Happiest Place on Earth...at least for dogs!

My heart is with all of you that have bid farewell for now to loved ones, it's our job to keep our happy theelings about them present and in our hearts.

# A LITTLE LENNY ENERGY

What an extraordinary Fall! There is so much to tell you about...

Last month, Lenny Kravitz played here in our little city. I have to tell you, I am so amazed that we get the great talents coming through that we do - I give thanks for that. We've had Elton John, David Bowie, Bryan Adams, Sting, Duran Duran, Billy Idol, Cher - just to name a few. When I was a kid growing up here, I never imagined my singing idols to grace our stage. Anyways, I'm just bragging - lol.

What I found really interesting about Lenny's concert is that amidst thousands of people and being on the floor only a few rows back from the stage is that I could feel that he didn't have the energy to be there. It was a great concert and it was great to see him so close and when I talked to others - they had no idea what I was talking about when I asked if they noticed his lack of energy. A few days later, he cancelled his remaining concerts due to illness.

Tapping into other peoples energy is natural to us all but it's amazing how often we don't do it...or don't admit it. What also tends to happen is that you get the feeling that people think you're weird (been there!) and then *you* start to think you're weird. Well, you're not! Pay attention to these signals - they exist and you're tapping into them. Honor them - they will serve you as doubt never does

*I am Passionate*

113

# RELATIONSHIPS

I am Tender

## VALENTINE'S DAY - BOOM OR BUST?

I tell ya - I have had some years where my Valentine's Days were absolute busts.

Happily, I can say that the last fourteen years of Valentine's have been wonderful (ever since Geoff and I got our belly buttons pierced on this day 14 years ago - long before it was fashionable - ha!)

Alright, TMI (too much information...) the point is that during that time when I was PG (pre-Geoff) I did three things that I KNOW attracted the right person to me - wanna know what they were?

Ya, I thought so!

1. I wrote a list of all the qualities of the person I wanted to spend time with;
2. I gave up looking for him (and, for heaven's sake, he lived right around the corner);
3. I started to have lots of fun.

Bingo, bango, bongo - he showed up. Try it!

For all of you in your boom times with your loved one - remember to appreciate EVERY bit of it!

# THE LAW OF ATTRACTION AND ATTRACTING YOUR DREAM RELATIONSHIP

What would it feel like to get up every day and be 'in love' with your partner? Day after day, month after month, year after year? Can you imagine that? Really take a moment and think about what that would be like for you.

What qualities would that partner have that you could be in love with every day? If you write this down right now and if I could fly around the world and look at everyone's answer - I could see something substantially different on every piece of paper.

The truth is that we're all looking for something different and that's why we're not attracted to everyone we come across.

Whatever you wrote down, has a frequency, an energy connected with it. To attract the partner with these qualities you need to connect with what it would feel like to be around a person with these qualities. Really connect with that feeling and how great it would be and be assured that person, whoever it is, is making their way to you.

Before I knew about the Law of Attraction, I had written down my own list. I went through a spell of kissing a lot of frogs

*I am Compassionate*

(well, not real frogs but some very wrong guys for me!) and remember lamenting to my friend Dawna about how lonely I was feeling. We would have our chats and she would always say 'you know....he's right around the corner'. Somehow this hope had redirected my energy from - 'where is he?' to 'yes, he's on his way!' It made all the difference and my energy did shift.

Funnily enough, Geoff, my sweetheart, actually did live right around the corner from me and I feel fortunate to say that I'm still in love thirteen and a half years later! I just asked and he says he feels the same and will be in love with me forever! :) Yahoo - what a sweetie, hey?!!! He possessed all the qualities I wrote down on my list BUT also didn't possess the qualities I forgot to write down. So, be thorough with your list! I lucked out and as it turns out the items I 'forgot' actually weren't that important.

Seek out couples who are in love - spend time with them if you can. Being in that kind of energy can literally rub off - or at the very least raise your standards! When you're around people that are truly in love - being around a partner or date that is not loving or respectful is such a contrast. Cherish this contrast, as it is very useful information that can help you to decide what you do and don't want.

# CAN I CHANGE SOMEONE ELSE'S FEELINGS?

*I'm a little confused. Based on a book that I am reading, the law of attraction works if I change the way I feel which in turn will change the way I think and bring me the happiness that my heart desires.*

*Now here is the question, If I change my feelings from I'm into him but he's not into me to something a little more positive such as I'm into him and he's into me how would this work? I mean I have changed my feelings to reflect something positive but he still has no interest in me. I don't understand how I can change someone else's feeling to reflect that of my state of mind. Is this possible at all? Should I be attempting to do this?*

---

Thanks for this question! First, the book you are reading is absolutely right! If you change the way you feel - your life will follow no matter what direction. If you change to feel good - your life will change and good things will happen to you. It is Law!! If you change to feel bad - eventually your life will change in that direction too. Ever have one of those days when you get up on the wrong side of the bed? Ya, it's kind of like that. The opposite is when you are having a day when you feel on top of the world and it seems like nothing can go wrong.

I'm going to take two angles on your question. First, if you like someone and you feel he's not into you - it's likely that you will perpetuate that. You'll do goofy things like look away if he looks at you or say something odd when he talks to you. Get the picture? It's easy enough to do - we give people the wrong impression all the time because we have already written a script in our head that we're not good enough and we act in a way that demonstrates that to the world.

So, if you change your thoughts to 'he'd be crazy not to be head over heels for me - you'll be putting out very different vibes and if he's the right match for you - he'll be knocking on your door before you know it.

The kicker is, if you noticed in the last sentence, I said 'if he's the right match'. The fact is, this guy might not be the right guy for you. I have no idea but what I do know is that I see so many people chasing after someone that they feel is the right match. I also see these people end up being hurt or in a relationship that is nowhere near what they really deserve. That's the thing about the Law of Attraction - it's about attraction - it's not called the Law of Chasing!!!

I would recommend you set your focus on the qualities of what you want in a relationship and not put the focus on any individual. If this guy deserves you and is the right match - once you start focusing on the qualities that will bring you joy - he'll show up.

I am Closer

Have you accessed your free bonus materials yet?
Go to www.theattractioninactionbook.com!

# HOW DO I DEAL WITH A LOVED ONE'S NEGATIVITY?

When it comes to questions about the Law of Attraction, the questions I receive the most from my audience are around how to deal with negativity of others. It seems many, many people have negative loved ones in their life that they feel are holding them back from their good. Don't you wish there was a pill for that?

What do you do when you're trying to change your own beliefs and own thought patterns so you have more hope and more expectancy of good things in your life? Gosh, it's hard enough being vigilant about what's going on for you never mind having to add other people's 'stuff' into the mix.

When people start to learn more about the Law of Attraction and how much impact our thoughts, feelings and beliefs have on the outcome of their life, they obviously start to try to monitor that more closely. Essentially, positive thoughts, feelings and beliefs create positive outcomes in one's life. Negative thoughts, feelings and beliefs create negative outcomes. Simple, right? Absolutely, this is a simple concept. Easy to implement? Well, not always.

This brings us back to our wanna-be positive person with the negative-nelly spouse or close family member. We've all been through this scenario where we are having a pretty good day.

We've been at home or at work doing our own thing and feeling pretty good about ourselves and our prospects and you connect with your loved one and BANG their mood or words immediately impact you. You've now gone from feeling pretty on top of the world to wanting to rip someone's face off. Not good. This shift has happened all because of the impact of this other person's mood or words. Now I'm going to shift that statement a tad and say this instead - this shift has happened all because of the impact *you let* this other person's mood or words have on you. Get it? It's a choice.

Why would we let someone else's words or moods or energy impact us when the effects can be so detrimental? For the most part, it's because we've learned this from our parents or caregivers. It really is a survival skill that has helped many people survive their childhood years. This behavior is also called co-dependency, but I'm not going to get into this here. The fact is, as we get older this survival skill becomes less useful and often harmful to our self-esteem. And, with Law of Attraction, succumbing to others bad moods only helps to ensure that the life that we truly want stays at bay.

How DO you deal effectively with someone else's negativity? There are a number of ways but let's explore one here that I have found works very effectively with situations where you know ahead of time that the person you will encounter is going to be negative.

This technique goes by a variety of names but all I want you to do is to imagine the situation you are about to go into and ask yourself this question....what is the best outcome I could imagine that I would like to have happen? Notice I'm not asking you to imagine the most likely outcome or even the best outcome considering the source. I want you to imagine YOUR best outcome.

I walked through this exercise with a woman who was about to go and meet her ex-husband to do the weekend kid exchange thing. As she describes, their interactions never go well and are always very strained and frustrating. She wanted that to change. I asked her to imagine the best outcome and, of course, to what she thought was possible. I egged her on and asked again for her best outcome. Next, she was to really imagine how incredible that would feel to have the outcome happen that she wanted to happen. We got her to stay in that moment for a bit and really feel the feelings. Not a hard process - quick and easy. When I next saw her she mentioned that her meeting with her ex was the most positive she had had in a long time and he even asked her why they were getting along so well!

Why did this happen? She shifted her energy and therefore everything else shifted. Simple Law of Attraction in practice. Try it out next time you're expecting a lousy encounter, my bet is that you'll have better results and less negativity.

# HE'S JUST NOT THAT INTO YOU....

Recently the movie based on the book 'He's just not that into you' came out to theaters. What gets me wondering is whether people will finally get the message.

As a girl growing up, I was always desperate to be loved. I always had boyfriends and had no problems around that except for one thing....many of my boyfriends were absolutely no good for me or my self-esteem.

Of course, I attracted that because I had low self-esteem. Then, one day in my late 20's or early 30's, everything changed. I stopped looking for love and started enjoying being with me and finding out what I wanted from my life.

When Geoff came into my life shortly thereafter, I was ready for him...or at least pretty ready. You see, he called when he said he was going to call. He looked thrilled to see me and he was nice to me and excited to introduce me to his friends.

What did I do? I kept looking for flaws - he was too good to be true, so much so that I almost started picking fights because I couldn't understand why he was so good to me and then I stopped. He was exactly what I had been hoping for but I had to grow into the person that could accept that level of love, sharing and intimacy. And I did, I just accepted that I was good enough

I am Thoughtful

to be treated well. Did you get that - I finally allowed myself to be treated well!!

Every week I get emails from people who want a particular person in their life - usually someone that has already been in their life and has moved on. The writer usually wants to know how to get that person back. (And yes, I am so guilty of this in my past!)

It breaks my heart because everyone deserves to have the 'Mr. Right' or 'Miss Right'. What ends up happening is that the focus of these writers is on what is no longer a match for them. That's a focus on lack, not love. Dr. Phil said it the best - your boyfriend or girlfriend should be treating you as the special person you really are (or something along those lines!). In any case, all of us deserve to be treated wonderfully and if someone in your life isn't treating you that way - they don't deserve to be in your life.

Get this - and especially for **Valentine's Day** - focus on the great times you had with the other person, focus on the qualities (not the person) that you loved and then focus on being good to yourself. If that person who is now gone is meant to be with you - they will be attracted back to you by the focus on the good stuff rather than the focus on getting them back. Truly, that rarely works out in the long run.

Also, get this....we all will move heaven and earth to be with the person we really want to be with and if someone is not doing that for you, don't make up excuses for them. They are not the right person for you and vice versa....period.

If you can do these few things and accept this new understanding into your consciousness you will turn a new page in your life and next Valentine's Day will ROCK!

I am understanding

## ATTRACTING AND KEEPING LOVE

If you are blessed enough to have a loved one in your life - remember to show them how much you appreciate them! (Step Five - Receive It and Appreciate It)

If you are patiently and expectantly waiting for the love of your life to show up in your life - share the day with people that you love. Remember, the more we can experience what we want (whether in real life or in our imagination) we move our self to a vibrational level that matches what we want and we end up attracting what we want that much faster.

# GOT THE OPPOSITE - I'M REALLY DOUBTING THE SECRET

Eventually, when using the Law of Attraction, there will be times when we get the exact, complete opposite of what we have been actively trying to attract. My gosh, why does that happen? One of my listeners has had this experience - read her email below.....

--------

*I will begin by apologizing beforehand, this is going to be a bit long. I know you must be a very busy person and probably get a million of these mails, but I pray that you will read my mail and be able to provide some much needed insight before I lose myself completely in these horrible feelings I have.*

*I first saw The Secret DVD a few weeks ago, and got a lot out of watching it. I started focusing on what I wanted and what I was grateful for. I spent a lot of time visualizing about my relationship with my boyfriend. I thought of us living together, getting married and all the things I wanted to do with him. I visualized the ring on my finger and us together growing old. I thought I was on the right track, but all of a sudden out of nowhere he broke up with me, saying that he felt like the spark had left our relationship over the past few weeks. I just lost my best friend and boyfriend of two years because of a few slow*

I am Friendly

129

*weeks, without warning or a chance for us to work through it. I'm sorry to go on like this, but I'm at a complete loss and feel devastated. I thought that I was on the right track but now I'm having doubts about The Secret. I've been trying to figure out what went wrong, maybe I didn't let go of my insecurities and doubt as much as I thought, or maybe I didn't focus on visualizing enough. My question is what can I do now, having tried using the law of attraction and getting the exact opposite of what I wanted? Should I continue to apply the law of attraction and hope that this is just a bump in the road rather than the end all of our relationship- or am I on the wrong track completely? What advice can you, as someone who has had success with the law of attraction, give me?*

*Where do I go from here? I still want him back and I simply cant believe this is the end of us- is there any hope? I'm not ready to give up on The Secret and the law of attraction, I do believe deep down it can work, I just can't seem to figure out how to make it work for me. I apologize again for the lengthy mail, I guess I'm just looking for some answers in this hole I've ended up in.*

*Again, sorry for the long mail, I hope you will answer my questions. Thank you for the site, it is a great resource and very motivational. I hope to see your reply on the site soon.*

Thank you for your email - sounds like you have been going through a very confusing time!! I can completely see how you could doubt all this Law of Attraction and The Secret stuff.

It's been a number of weeks since you sent this email and I'm curious to see where things are at for you - I hope you send me an email back letting me know.

Here's my take on this - be assured that you're definitely NOT doing something wrong!! In fact, you did everything right and the universe responded - with bells on!

Sometimes I think there should be a disclaimer when using any new ways of thought - like, be careful what you wish for!!! I know, you're probably, saying 'Whaaaat....? Karen, did you not just read my email?! I certainly did not wish for this!"

Yup, I know, however, what happens often is that when we learn a new way of being and thinking - things around us change sometimes very drastically and in the exact opposite direction to what we thought we were manifesting. Sound familiar? This process is often referred to as chemicalization. It's a phase where your environment drastically changes in response to your intent, your vibration, your feelings.

Time will definitely tell on where this lands for you, but you started putting out some very strong and very deliberate vibrations and good for you!! There is nothing as satisfying as becoming crystal clear about what you want. Now, whether or not you said anything to your boyfriend - be assured - he felt the change and he reacted.

The things you desired may not be a match to where he's at and that's why he, 'out of the blue', ended things. Or, he may have felt those vibrations emanating from you so strongly that he temporarily bolted. He may become comfortable with those feelings and come back because it is a match to him (it was just a quick leap in vibration that he wasn't expecting) and you could very well see your creation coming true. As I say, time will tell. The thing is - in order for you to have what you really desired as you wrote in your email - things had to change and that future result is either with him or someone even better.

You have a couple of choices here - keep deliberately using the law of attraction in the way you were previously and he'll either come around or someone who is a direct match to your desires will. If you decide to hell with the things that you asked for - you just want him back regardless...... use the Law of Attraction to imagine what your life was like and how good you felt in the state you were in previously. Either way, it may not be an easy choice.

You did mention something about insecurities and doubts and I wonder if these were about your relationship or yourself. If they were about the relationship - could be you were tapping into that vibrational level but didn't allow yourself to really admit that maybe things were not as good a match as you were hoping.

In the end, we can't create for anyone else but ourselves and either the people around us match where we're going or they won't and they will fall away from our lives. It can be tough going through this as it doesn't seem to make any sense and seems to be the exact opposite of what we were asking for.

Chemicalization can happen in any situation we're trying to attract - whether it's love, money, a job or a new home - when we get clear - the things that don't match will fall away and we'll sometimes end up in far more dire circumstances than what we started with. The Universe, God, Allah – Source Energy - is responding positively to your requests! It's- not reprimanding you for being so bold as to ask for something better. Remember that! It's always darkest just before the dawn.

I am There

# FRIENDS AND THE LAW OF ATTRACTION

I don't know about you but sometimes I'm perplexed by the people that wander in and out of my life. Sometimes I'm seriously very glad some move on and some leave me scratching my head wondering what went wrong?

The fact is that we attract people that are a match at some level. When we no longer match at some level - we move on - easy as that but it can be hard to let go of the one's we really like!

# WANTS TO ATTRACT MORE FRIENDS

*Dear Karen,*

*I am an 11 year old guy. I am pretty successful in class and the law of attractions, but when it comes to making friends it is a little harder. i pretty much understand the law of attraction but i cant attract more people around me. I pretty much use all the tips you gave me but when it comes to making friends it is harder for me to use the law of attraction.*

*Why is that?*

-------------------------

I love getting emails from kids - I think it's so cool and I'm so excited that they know this stuff early in life - I think the future of our world is in great hands if the kids are figuring this out now!!!

Thanks so much for writing!!! Most of the time with the Law of Attraction - if we're not getting what we want - it can be because of a variety of any one of these things:

1. We're not really that focused on it and don't have a lot of energy around it and so the Universe picks up from us that it isn't as important to us as other things in our life....

2.  We get in our own way of allowing what we want.  We ask for it and then spend our energy wondering where 'it' is.  By doing that - we are noticing the lack of the friends being around and the more we focus on that - the more we get of that - a lack of friends.....

3.  Sometimes we create too many rules about what something 'should' be like and so we don't notice when what we're looking for is standing right in front of us....

4.  Going back to allowing - sometimes we don't feel good enough about ourselves to believe we can be a good friend or worthy of having friends.  I think the world of kids is a lot more difficult than it used to be and feeling self confident can be a tough road.  Believe me, you're worth having as a friend and everyone needs at least one friend!!!

5.  Sometimes and I'm reaching here, there just isn't a good match for a friend in your vicinity - this could definitely be true but I think it's more likely that there some level of not allowing your friend to appear..... 99 times out of 100 - what's getting in the way is us not allowing the good to come into our life.  But I've got some suggestions!

For everything you want in life - give it away or BE what you want, first. What this means is - if you want a friend - BE a friend first. Give your friendship away - be 'there' for someone. If you want someone to talk to - be a listener first. This IS the Law of Attraction - BE what you want first and you'll attract it. Give it away and you'll attract more.

Everyone wants to be heard - so listen - I bet you'll find lots of friends around you quickly. What you put out comes back ten-fold!!!

I am Secure

## MY FRIENDS ARE NOT LIKE ME AT ALL!

*Hi, my question to you is why am I attracting friends that are so opposite to me? I am so organized, my friends are not. I am not a procrastinator my friends are. I like to be active my friends don't. I am fit my friends are not. I am not a material person my friends are. What is it that I am doing to attract all the wrong people into my life? That goes for girl friends and male friends. I am a 50ish woman and I have no significant other and boy would I love to have that part of my life full. Please help!!!!!!*

*C*
*from NY*

———————

Hello to my friend in NY!! My guess is that there is some common ground here. Do you have fun with these friends? Do you talk with them? Do they listen to you? Do you work together?

Absolutely, without one doubt - there is some commonality - only you can identify what it is though. Our friends don't have to be just like us - in fact, that would probably be quite boring after a bit.

Take a few moments and look for the things you like about your friends and that will probably be your common attractor. If you want to attract new friends with the qualities you have - start appreciating those qualities in others (even in the friends who don't seem to have those qualities). Appreciate those qualities in yourself too that you want to attract.

Remember, if you're thinking something's missing - it's not going to change if you're focusing your energy on that missing piece. You'll just get more of 'missing'. Focus on seeing what you want present all around you. Look - I bet you'll find it!

I am Confident

# FINDING AND KEEPING THE LOVE YOU TRULY DESERVE

Alright, it's just about Valentine's Day and you are on either one side of the fence or the other. You are part of the haves or have nots. Most of us want to be on the 'haves' side and some of us are trying to keep our 'have' status. This article is for both of you creatures. :)

You deserve to find or keep the love you deserve - so, what are you doing about it?

If you don't have the love in your life that you want - use the Law of Attraction to get it. Do you find you keep ending up with the same kind of schmucks and schmuckettes? Well, there is a reason for that - you're not using the Law of Attraction deliberately. Do you spend time going over and over in your mind what went wrong with the last 'love of your life' and have you been focusing on what a strike to your self-esteem they were? Guess what!? You're well on your way to finding an exact behavioral match with different skin on the outside.

Get out of that rut, now! Start being deliberate about the Law of Attraction and start focusing on what you DO want. Start by creating a list of all the character traits you want in your partner. Reframe the negatives into a positive statement (remember what you focus on grows) - for example, if your last partner was demeaning to you in public ask for this - "My ideal partner for me treats me with love and respect at all times". Or, if you had a partner that cheated on you - write down on your list - "My ideal partner has eyes only for me" instead of "My ideal partner doesn't cheat". The universal energy only picks up and reflects back on the feeling of the words (cheat) and doesn't hear negatives (doesn't).

I used to think it would be great to have a very good looking male version of my best friend. Naw, it really wasn't weird! I was focusing on all the fun things my best friend and I would do together and thought it would be great to have a love who would want to do the same kinds of things plus be my love! It worked! It can work for you, too!

Now, for those of you who do have someone in your life... How do you keep them? How do you keep that fire going?

I've seen relationship after relationship fall into some pretty predictable patterns where partners fall out of appreciation for each other and that might as well be the death-knell of the relationship.

So many of us start to focus on the nit-picky things in life and get frustrated with our partner. You can find terrible things about the most wonderful person in the world if you look and you can find wonderful things about the worst. It's all about what YOU choose to focus on. What you focus on - you get. If you focus on the other's faults - you literally cannot see the loving person you decided to be with.

Your brain works to prove you right. If you have an opinion or are seeking something - your brain will help you find it.

So the question is, do you want to see a wonderful, loving person across from you who is perfect in their non-perfection or an uncaring, stupid idiot who just isn't even close to perfect? What you look for - you'll find.

If you're in a great relationship - keep focusing on what makes it great.

If you're not in a great relationship - start changing your mind. Start looking for the positive aspects in that person.

# WANT LOVE – GOT A GREAT JOB INSTEAD

*A few months ago, I started to use the Law of Attraction to focus on manifesting the love relationship that I really want (and not just a relationship - I wanted this to be the love-of-my-life relationship), and I was getting excited and feeling really positive when I do it. I was focusing on qualities I was really looking for (I even made up a list), and added thoughts like "it's just around the corner", and I really felt good and positive about it. I really believed it, like it was really truly going to happen any time soon.*

*Well, the love relationship hasn't manifested yet, but what happened was I got a fantastic job that I never ever would have dreamed of having, and it all happened so fast. In fact when I left the interview I didn't really think I was going the get the job, but I got a call back the very next day and was told they really wanted to hire me. Wow! I was elated, and I thought this is great and it came from out of nowhere.*

*I thought I was so lucky, and then I thought it must be the Law of Attraction, but I wasn't focusing on a new job (although it is a fantastic one); I was focusing on a love relationship. Is it possible that when we focus on getting one thing, that we end up getting something else? Or does this mean this is just the first step to manifesting the love relationship I have been focusing on?*

I am Smart

143

---

Thank you for this question - it's a fabulous observation!  Ever heard of the saying 'the better it gets - the better it gets..."?  This is an example of the Law of Attraction at work.  When we're feeling good and getting excited about the possibilities of our life - we start to attract more good things.

If you can maintain this high vibration, you'll find more and more opportunity.  Also, it seems that you've been very clear about what you want and so the Universe is delivering.  I wouldn't be the least bit surprised if the love-of-your-life relationship shows up soon.  You might meet the person at work - they might be someone you work with or someone your company deals with.  You might meet them on the way to or from work or you might meet them through someone new you get to know at work.  Now, isn't this just incredibly exciting?  If you can make a fun game of this - you'll keep your vibration high.  (oooh, was that him...or him....or him.... or her.....or her..... or her.....!?)

Sometimes the expectation is that when we ask for something, that the thing we ask for is going to fall out of the sky and land right in front of us.  The fact is, if you want something to be different in your life, you have to be different first.

So, don't be surprised that when you ask for something and start getting excited about it that a current of change will start to occur in your life. The current may be really obvious or it may be discreet - it may look great - it may look awful - but if you notice change happening - be sure that what you've asked for is on it's way.

I am Soothing

## BABY, COME BACK...

*Hi Karen,*

*I have been in a very passionate but short lived relationship with a woman I truly believed I would marry and have children with. I felt her in every part of my body, which was quite remarkable as I have never felt like this before with any of my previous relationships. But before I met her, I had a dream of my ideal person, who standing with me on the edge of where land air and water meet. In my dream we stood for what seemed like a long time, not saying anything to each other.*

*A couple of weeks went by and I met this woman at a party, and when we spoke I remembered my dream. We started seeing each other, but then she kept saying things to me about me taking my ex, who I had been with for 18 years. I said we were friends and there was nothing going on between us, although we (my ex and I) lived in the same house. She wanted me to move in with her in the few weeks, but I was wasn't concerned everything was moving too fast too quickly.*

*Since then we have broken up due to the untold number of arguments that have been raised, mainly due to my ex. I moved out my house, and into a smaller one. Recently I have been thinking on the LOA and tried an experiment, and asked, please bring "her" back into my life.*

*Well sure enough she came back, but she came back with the same attitude as when we broke up. We sent emails to each other, but seen each other for nearly 1 year. I would like her back, but I am not sure how to ask, using the LOA, because I don't really want her to come back with the same attitude as when she left.*

*Is there anything I can do to formulate my requests effectively? We are now like two bird sitting on a rooftop at either end, waiting as to who will make the first move.*

*Many thanks*
*Cole*

I am Courageous

---

Thanks for your question Cole! Isn't it amazing when we are able to use the Law of Attraction so well that what we've been asking for shows up!? Being able to be crystal clear about what you want (and don't want) is so important in this process otherwise we do end up with results we hadn't anticipated. You want to make sure that you follow the Five Steps System I've identified.

Once you get clear, the asking begins and we're asking 24/7 so the challenge is not so much in formulating the request (although that *is* important) as it is in keeping our mind off 'what is' or 'what was'.

As long as we keep going back to 'the reality' of the situation we'll stay stuck and keep attracting the same thing because that's where our focus remains. Wherever our energy is focused - reciprocal energy will respond and materialize.

There are a few things I would recommend to get started:

- Get really clear about what you do and don't want in a relationship and focus on that
- Be vigilant about where your focus is daily
- Review where your energy and focus is at around your 'ex' and get help by checking in with friends that you know will tell you the truth - ask them if they feel you're still attached

# ATTRACTING LOVE...A REVIEW

*Hi Karen,*

*Thank you so much for all of the podcasts and for your LOA tips! I really feel that you have helped me better my life in so many ways! I wanted to ask you something though. I wanted to ask you why your podcasts and email tips so rarely talk about attracting love, relationships and romance? From hearing you speak, it seems that this is clearly an area that you have manifested a great deal of happiness and could really teach us. For one of the most important things to seek in life it just seems to take a back seat sometimes to money, time and even weight loss on your podcasts. Do you have any episodes planned to cover this? Thank you so much!*

*- April*

---

Hi April - you're right; I have been focusing on money a lot lately. I tend to write about what is most in my face from both my audience questions and from what we all tend to be hit by with the media. Thanks for this email (and a note to all of you have a question about other topics - send them in!!).

I remember the days when finding the love of my life was THE most important issue in my life. Money was good to have but finding love was paramount. I still feel the same today - money is great but my Number 1 Priority is my love, Geoff.

How DO you use the Law of Attraction to attract love?

As many of you know - I recommend the Five Steps for everything and you should review the steps and use them but I'll share one particular strategy. (there are many! ;))

If you haven't done this already - look back in your past relationships, love and otherwise, and make a list of any recurring themes (problems, challenges, traits). Is there some recurring aspects of past relationships that you would like to eliminate?

It often happens that we repeat patterns in ALL of our relationships, we attract what we know. We also often repeat our parents relationship (yikes for some of us!). Take a close look - you might be surprised.

This is part of the first step, to become aware, this can often uncover one of the things that blocks us. How does it block us? If we have had some difficult relationships and we aren't sure why they happened, we could be blocking ourselves from moving forward. We don't want to attract more of the same so better not to attract anything at all. Sound familiar? By starting to uncover some of the past challenges that we have attracted, we can start to become aware of how we may have attracted them in the first place and change our thoughts, feelings and beliefs. When we can do that - we change everything.

Start here - I promise it will be enlightening.

I am a Miracle

# MONEY

I am Fancy

## YOUR MONEY BLUEPRINT

If you listen to my podcasts - you know I just posted my Interview with a Multi, Multi, Multi Millionaire T. Harv Eker. It was a great interview and I'll be posting more of the interview in oncoming weeks. I just got my copy of Secret of the Millionaire Mind and truly, if you want to attract more money into your life - this book has some great information.

I especially like the section on 'Your Money Blueprint', when Harv and I talked during my podcast, some of the references he made to our money blueprint got me thinking more about where my ideas about money come from. Now, I had done this before but not in this way. I have reset my blueprint prior but I'll need more help setting it to where I'd really like to be - that's why I'll be attending the Millionaire Mind Intensive in Vancouver in October.

This past weekend I had the pleasure of meeting some people who have worked directly with Harv and they are the epitome of success, confidence and values-based business people! They didn't know I had interviewed Harv and it was a testimonial to me of the power of Harv's work.

# WHY IS EVERYTHING FOR SALE?

*Precious Karen,*

*I LOVE YOU*

*I am sending out this to you as you are a UNIVERSE!!!!!*

*Please help me.*

*Everything is for sale in the universe, why is that???*

*I am pretty much surprised to have knowledge of LAW OF ATTRACTION, MANIFESTATIONS, CREATIONS, LOVE, JOY, HAPPINESS, FREEDOM etc......*

*Sad thing is the people who know the secret to APPLY the right TECHNIQUE to make their wishes come true, CHARGE FOR THIS KNOWLEDGE to deliver it to other poor, needy, unworthy, unsuccessful and in the dirt people. They charge money!!!!*

*Did all PROPHETS make money to share this knowledge to poor and hungry people???*

*Did all great people ask for money to let other people live the life of their dreams????*

*Why is everything for sale Karen????*

*I am also suffering a lot from joblessness, financially broke very badly.*

*To get to the top most position in life I need to learn and apply the all laws working. Tell me how can I purchase the application process to be a free human being. What you can do for me is to please call universe and manifest and create for me.*

*I am Romantic*

*Let me tell you what I want:*

*I want a job as good as beyond my expectations, Financially SOUND, secure with a company maintained CAR in order to support myself, my family and all others needing.*

*I want to be FREE*

*I want to be a MASTER OF ALL UNIVERSAL LAWS*

*I want to be rich, rich, rich to get whatever I want.*

*I want to see the whole world, the strangest most places.*

*I want to meet great people including YOU, the great KAREN.*

*Please please please Karen, do it for me Please....*

*Warm Regards*

*W*

---

Hi W - thank you for the kind words and the great question!!

First things first - I cannot create for you! You are the only one that can create your life and by the looks of it - you're pretty clear on what you do want. You've asked - the Universe has heard - now we just need to work on your faith that it's all coming to you!

You can start on that belief by starting to appreciate what you have NOW. You have created all the good that you have in your life - start being aware of that and focus on it and give thanks for it. A great thing to do is keep a Gratitude Journal and this can be as fancy as getting a special book just for this purpose or finding a piece of paper and writing down at the end of each day all the things in your life that you have to be grateful for. Sometimes this is a stretch for us but it is totally possible. There is ALWAYS something to be grateful for - ALWAYS - you just have to look.

You say you have a family - that's something to grateful for! You have the ability to drive a car - that's something to be grateful for! You have had use of a computer to send this email with - that's something to be grateful for! Start paying attention to what you have and loving it and the things you want will start to come. You just have to believe it's possible and believe you're worthy.

Now, as far as your question about why everything is for sale. That's a great question and I want to give you an uncomplicated answer - so here goes....

Everything is for sale because everything for sale has value to someone. Value is just energy - like everything else and at this point in time - we trade value energy for money energy. It's all just energy we are exchanging.

People charge for this information because they have mouths to feed and bills to pay and they paid money to acquire this information. And there isn't a darn thing wrong with that. You see, most people that share and profit from this information do so because they have an intense desire to help others and make the process of learning easier than they found it. Some of these people also give away a lot, too. What goes around comes around - it's all the Law of Attraction.

Interesting that you mentioned the Prophets - I don't know enough to know whether they received money directly for the information they relayed but they had to eat and clothe themselves and travel to spread their knowledge - that happened somehow, through other's donations or support. There was a trading of energy of value of that information for support.

Be okay with people profiting from the value they offer and you will attract the riches you want faster. We all deserve to be rich - we just haven't all figured that out yet.

Last thing I want to address - you mentioned 'the poor, needy, unworthy, unsuccessful... and I just want to reinforce that NO ONE is unworthy - not one human being on the face of this planet. So if you were, by chance, describing yourself - KNOW THIS - YOU ARE WORTHY, DESERVING, SUCCESSFUL AND RICH just by being a being on this planet. Once you KNOW that it will be so.

Thank you W - you're on the right path!

# WHAT HAPPENS IN VEGAS ...

Last week Geoff and I went to Vegas for the World Market
Furniture Show as Geoff is in the high-end furniture business.

I love checking out furniture and accessories! We found some
absolutely beautiful lines to add to the store.

Did you know that many people spend as much on furniture
purchases as some people do in buying a house? I have to tell
you, when I saw my first $10K couch about ten years ago - well,
I didn't understand. Why would someone spend that kind of
money on a couch? We now have a similar couch in our home.
I tell you this not to boast (not at all!) but to let you know that
anything is possible. Did we focus and dream about the couch?
Not at all, in fact, this is one of those things that fall into place as
you get clear about the kind of life you would like to live. We
want to live a life that is cloaked in beautiful things. It's
automatic attraction.

How do you do this? (Ya, I know the couch might not be your
thing - but this idea is transferable to anything you want to attract
into your life)

If you're wanting to attract wealth into your life - you need to
start expanding your boundaries of what's possible and normal
for rich people. You have to take yourself to the next level by
broadening your experience and your beliefs. And, you need to

I am Youthful

159

also start without trying to figure out the 'how's' of how this can all happen for you - just focus on the end result. The 'how's' will fall into place.

And, did you know that you can do all this and still be a spiritual being and do good for others? Why not?

# URGENTLY NEEDS MONEY...!

*Hi*

*I need money urgently as my husband and I have 3 children attending university next year, one doing her honours, and the other 2 will be first year students.*

*We both have lost just about everything materially.*

*We both have wonderful opportunities to make money, as we are both graduates, attractive, and people like us. But we just don't see the money in our bank accounts.*

*Any advice?*

*R*

---

Hi R - whew!! This can feel like a tough, tough position to be in. The feelings of lack of money can be so crushing and so distracting that you couldn't see daylight if someone put you smack dab in the middle of the desert. I understand. I think most of the population could relate that feeling one time or another.

There are two things you said - 'we have wonderful opportunities to make money, as we are both graduates, attractive, and people like us' - that's perfect and that's what you want to focus on.

Your second sentence was 'but we just don't see the money in our bank accounts.' - that's exactly what you don't want to focus on.

Your job is to pull out all stops and focus on your first statement. Do everything you can to remember that the Universe is the source of all your good. Get into a great feeling place and then act on inspiration. Go with your gut. If someone offers an opportunity that doesn't even remotely look like an opportunity - go back and reassess.

I read a crucial statement the other day by Mike Dooley that changed my perspective instantly in that moment (you see, even when you know this stuff - it's way to easy to get caught up in the emotions of something lousy - so you always need to have ways to pull yourself out of that in a moments notice) and the statement was this...

*'The reason that some of your thoughts haven't yet become things is because other thoughts of yours have.'*

Now, in a dark moment, is a time of opportunity even though it doesn't look like that at all. Look for those hidden gems.

Another statement I ALWAYS use is 'when the going gets tough, ask for more stuff' (thanks Tom and Penelope Pauley). Asking for more stuff just tells the Universe that you know that lack and limitation is not your path. Be bold!

# THIS IS WHAT I'M TALKIN' ABOUT!

*I want let you know for last few months I keep getting a strong intuitive feeling my life is being successfully being manifested by law of universe and will received all the things I desire such as:*

*Dream home in Seattle, Washington by next month paid in full more than afforded all the amenities and luxury..*

*Maintaining excellent health, happiness, dreams auto machine, and many more ..*

*Every day when I wake I want to show gratitude the universe for all already fulfilling all of my dreams and wishes..*

*Although I'm mentally preparing moved to the Seattle, Washington and prepare have "Thanksgiving in "Seattle dream home with new friends and People I met in short time ..*

*Two weeks from now I prepare to go visit my dream home by during a final walk through with a real estate agent in Mid-October..*

*I just feel I'll more than financial assets to buy all the items I want without a doubt...*

I am Generous

*I can't listen what other thinking Why I'm leaving Norfolk, VA from a affordable "Town home" to move the Northwest..*

*I just feel a strong intuitive sense just be prepare to move when the universe instructed ..*

---

Sam sent this email to me last Fall and it's this kind of faith in one's self and one's feelings that I talk about in many of my tips letters.

Getting to that feeling of KNOWING that what you want is coming is the feeling you want to achieve.

Think back to a time when you absolutely KNEW without one ounce of doubt that what you thought about was going to happen - and then it happened. This could have been a good event or a bad event. Now try and remember what your reaction was to that thought coming to fruition....

Here's how the self-talk often goes...

**If it was a good event** - 'Ah, it was just luck - the right place at the right time, but I thought it might happen'

**If it was a bad event** - 'I KNEW that was going to happen! I just knew something *bad* was going to happen!'

Sound familiar?

Start acknowledging that luck and law of attraction are synonymous. Start acknowledging that the sense of KNOWING. I mean really, really KNOWING (which shouldn't be a feeling that isn't laced with fear) is also synonymous with the law of attraction. This is important because as soon as you can start acknowledging it you can start using it to your advantage.

I am Bountiful

# RECESSION BUSTING

I was listening to CNN the other night and as the talk swirled on about the potential of a recession in the US - one of the things that perked my ears up was that one of the experts talked about how mindset will have an effect on this economy and it's outcome.

Wow!! I knew that was a Law of Attraction nugget I was going to hold on to! I believe each and every one of us has the ability to turn this impending recession on its head. In fact, I'll go as far to say that we have a responsibility to do just that.

Remember, the worse it gets - the worse it gets just because that's where our focus is. The negative media attention just reinforces this aspect - unless we decide to stop listening.

Sometimes it's crucial to our well-being to turn off the damn news so we can actually develop our own thoughts and feelings about a situation. And, I love Anderson Cooper as much as the next person but you do have the power to turn the channel away from his ever-so trustworthy face. Just do it for a week - see how you feel. Maybe we'll start an AC360 recovery support group. ;)

Now, I know people are going through difficulties with the mortgage crisis and some people are losing their homes. That is

a real shame. Their job now is to find some opportunity out of
all of this mess.

For the rest of us who are living in a shadow of a 'potential'
recession, do you notice how the talk of a recession has helped
you to make different spending decisions? That's Law of
Attraction at work.

If you believe in the Law of Attraction - you know what to do.
Start imagining the elements of a healthy economy - that you,
your family and your neighbors have great jobs - healthy
incomes. If we can start to focus on the good that's around us -
we start to have faith in what we see rather than what we hear in
the media. It's at that point that the economy starts to turn
around. YOU have the power - it all starts with a thought.

I am Inquisitive

## NOTE FROM A FUTURE MILLIONAIRE

*Hello! I just wanted to share something with you that i know you could appreciate. I came across "The Secret", when it was presented on Oprah. I went out and bought the book read it and started to apply the information to my life. I wrote down many affirmations, i even recorded my affirmations onto my computer, then downloaded them to my iPod, and every chance i had my headphones were in my ears.*

*Part of one of my Mantras was" I have MILLIONS of dollars in the bank". So, any way one day I'm sitting at the train station waiting for my train. But a friend of mine had made plans for us to hang out, we hadn't hung out in a while and all week was so looking forward to it. So i called to confirm, and he cancelled. I was Livid, because it happens so much. So I'm sitting there fuming after our conversation, boiling! It took me less than ten seconds before i realized i need to refocus, that negative energy into positive energy, because i recognized the energy was STRONG!!!*

*So I took a deep breath closed my eyes, head towards the sky, and began chanting to myself, "I have MILLIONS of dollars in the bank! I have MILLIONS of dollars in the bank!! Over and over again. After about a minute or so I stopped opened my eyes looked down between my feet. At first I thought I was a $20 bill, so I picked it up and after further inspection, it was an oversized* *fake MILLION dollar bill! Granted it wasn't real, but here I am chanting about my MILLIONS in the bank. And here it is literally at my feet.*

*To me that was the universe confirming my power, and it confirmed that my real MILLIONS are on the way. Of course that bill is now on my vision board, that I see every day. I just wanted to share that with you, and want you to share this story with others on their same vibration.*

*I also wanted to say I enjoy listening to you podcast, and thank you.*

*Future MILLIONAIRE!!*

---

Thanks for this email!

I thought I would share this email with you because this is a great example of a few things:

- turning around strong emotion effectively (this is such an important thing to do!)
- acknowledging what we've created
- Remaining positive (how many people would see the fake bill and have a negative reaction?) and using the gift as a touchstone to create the real thing.

*I am Determined*

If we pay attention, we likely have opportunity daily to do what Antonio did. I challenge you - this week - pay attention to when you have strong negative emotions and try to refocus there on the spot. Then, send me your stories!!

# IT'S ALL ABOUT MINDSET

I was teaching one of my classes this week - Seven Steps to Success and I was reminded about how oblivious we can be when our mind isn't open when we're faced with information so completely divergent from what we know.

A gentleman in my class could not conceive of a reality that was different than the one he was living at this moment. He truly felt his course was set and what he was living was as good as it gets. I am not for one moment criticizing this very sweet fellow - he is following his path and no one can fault him for that.

What it did do for me was to remind me and reinforce for me that it is so important to keep expanding beyond our ideas about what we think is limiting us.

For example, I have had a dollar amount in my mind for a monthly income that I think was incredible and far beyond what I've ever earned before - it was astronomical (in my mind at the time) and I certainly didn't know anyone personally who made that kind of money. But, as I paid attention, I found more and more people who were earning that money - easily.

Then, I met someone last November who, very matter-of-factly, said to me - you could be earning monthly what you used to make in a year. I have to tell you, for as much as I work at expanding and moving beyond my resistance, my resistance came up - BIG TIME! As it turned out, many of the people in the room I was in were doing just that.

You know, it's not just about money - it's about what we think we're capable of or worth. If you're not healthy and can't even remember what it's like to feel good - look hard for others that have beat what you're fighting. Chances are they're out there and are trying to share their story with others.

The fellow in my class this week reminded me that it is so important to keep pushing our boundaries because if we do - we'll be living a life that is beyond anything we could ever imagine. How incredible would that be?

# IS YOUR PASSION PAYING?

Do what you love and the money will come!  Right?  Sure!
However, the money might not show up in the way you expect it
to.  In fact, the money might NOT actually come from what
you're passionate about.

What!?  I don't understand, Karen!  I've been hearing this phrase
for quite some time now and I believe it!

Absolutely!  AND, you should keep believing it!  With Law of
Attraction, if you're feeling great doing something you
absolutely love - the money WILL come - you'll be attracting
abundance just by feeling good.  It just might not come in the
way you expect it or in the time frame you want (but the timing
has more to do with your allowing process).

I'll illustrate what I mean by answering this great question I
received a few months ago, I'm going to answer IN CAPS within
the body of the question as there are so many great points.....

I am Interested

**FOLLOWED DREAMS BUT.....?**

*Hello Karen from Venezuela and congratulations on your podcasts and webpage!* A GREAT BIG THANK YOU FROM ME - K.!

*About two years ago my girlfriend and her mom began to talk to me about co-creation and I thought they were crazy. However, ever since I saw The Secret, it all became crystal clear, and I'm honestly a true believer in TLOA. However, I have a challenge for you.* BRING IT!! :) *You mentioned in a podcast the importance of passion and having passion for the things we do, or focus on activities we are passionate about. Well, precisely two years ago I was (and had been for a while) a well paid executive at a large multinational firm, but my true passion was for cooking, music and playing tennis. So it was the weekends mostly when I felt fulfilled since it was then when I got to cook, play music and play tennis. About a year and a half ago,  I decided to 'follow my dreams' and 'focus on what I'm passionate about' and quit my job to open a restaurant, and began to focus more as well on the music and the tennis.* THAT'S GREAT!!! I WONDER, WERE YOU ABLE TO REALLY ENJOY AND APPRECIATE DOING ALL
THE THINGS YOU LOVE? IT WOULD BE INTERESTING TO BE ABLE TO ASK YOU TO GO BACK AND REMEMBER WHAT FEELINGS YOU WERE HAVING AT THE TIME. WERE YOU ECSTATIC? WORRIED?

DOUBTFUL? HAVING THE TIME OF YOUR LIFE? WHAT SIDE OF THE TEETER-TOTTER DID THE BULK OF YOUR FEELINGS LIE - ON THE POSITIVE SIDE OR THE NEGATIVE SIDE? *Well, the restaurant failed and is losing money despite me pouring my heart and soul into it, and music and tennis don't bring in any paychecks (I've been training 2 hours a day for the past year and the best I might get to is to the best of the amateur categories here in Venezuela, where tournaments don't pay money to winners.* ARE YOU HAVING FUN? IF SO - KEEP DOING IT! IF YOU CAN'T MAKE MONEY AT PLAYING TENNIS - PERHAPS OTHER OPPORTUNITIES WILL AVAIL THEMSELVES IN A WAY YOU COULD HAVE NEVER THOUGHT! *And with the music, I bought the equipment, and I spend hours in the studio producing, yet record labels don't like my songs)* AGAIN, ARE YOU HAVING FUN? KEEP AT IT - THERE ARE COUNTLESS, COUNTLESS STORIES OF PEOPLE WHO KEPT AT IT AND BECAME PHENOMENALLY SUCCESSFUL. IT JUST DOESN'T ALWAYS SHOW UP IMMEDIATELY OR IN THE TIME FRAME YOU WISH. *So now I'm back to looking for a job since I've had to live off my savings throughout this period and can't stop thinking about the scene from 'Devil Wears Prada' when the kids toast to 'jobs that pay the rent'.* SURE, NOT QUITE WHAT YOU EXPECTED BUT IS THERE SOMETHING YOU CAN DO TO EARN MONEY AND KEEP HAVING FUN DOING WHAT YOU'RE

*I am Marvellous*

DOING?  THIS IS THE MOST OPPORTUNE TIME TO
THINK OUT OF THE BOX!!  YOU LOVE TENNIS AND
MUSIC AND COOKING - IS THERE A WAY TO CREATE
SOME KIND OF ONLINE BUSINESS AROUND THIS?
NOW IS THE TIME TO JUMP OUT OF TRADITIONAL
THINKING.  I HIGHLY RECOMMEND A BOOK BY
TIMOTHY FERRISS CALLED 'THE 4-HOUR WORK WEEK'.
I'LL PUT A LINK ON MY WEBPAGE.  THIS GUY IS MY
VERY NON-TRADITIONAL HERO!!

*So I admit the restaurant was poorly located.... but even so, and
more related to the music and tennis, isn't there an issue of
ABILITY to do things here?  I mean, I might love making music
and playing tennis but what if I'm not a gifted musician or tennis
player?* I THINK IF YOU ASK MANY 'GIFTED' ATHLETES
AND MUSICIANS - THEIR GIFT REALLY IS THEIR
PASSION TO IMPROVE THEIR ABILITY.  I'LL USE
HOCKEY GREAT, WAYNE GRETZKY, (SORRY, I KNOW
HOCKEY IS LIKELY NOT A GREAT EXAMPLE TO USE
FOR A VENEZUELAN FRIEND! BUT IT'S THE BEST
EXAMPLE I KNOW OF) HE PRACTICED DAY IN DAY
OUT AS A KID FOR HOURS AND HOURS - HE WAS
TOTALLY ABSORBED BY THIS SPORT.  I SEEM TO
REMEMBER THAT THE STORY GOES THAT HE
ACTUALLY HAD A 'STYLE' THAT WOULD LEAD ONE
TO BELIEVE THAT HE WOULDN'T BE SUCCESSFUL.

BUT, FROM MY PERSPECTIVE, HE WAS A GIFTED
ATHLETE BECAUSE HE HAD AN ALL-CONSUMING
PASSION. SO ABILITY PLAYS IN TO THE EQUATION IN
DIRECT PROPORTION TO ONE'S DRIVE TO IMPROVE
SKILL. WHILE I BELIEVE WE ALL HAVE ACCESS TO
THIS KIND OF DRIVE AND PASSION, I KNOW MOST OF
US DON'T ACCESS IT. *How do you find the balance or bridge
the gap between what you truly love to do and what you're born
to do (physically, ability wise). The big bucks from TLOA have to
come from somewhere, millionaire checks are not mailed in no
matter how hard you focus on it and desire it.* I GUESS MY
QUESTION WOULD BE TO YOU, MY WONDERFUL
FRIEND (THANK YOU SO MUCH FOR THIS QUESTION!)
IS 'DO YOU HAVE TO HAVE MILLIONAIRE CHECKS
COMING IN TO DO WHAT YOU LOVE TO DO?' FOR
SOME REASON, MOST OF US THINK WE HAVE TO BE A
MILLIONAIRE OR AT LEAST QUITE WEALTHY IN
ORDER TO DO WHAT WE LOVE ON AN ON-GOING
BASIS. THE FACT IS, WE MOSTLY JUST HAVE TO GIVE
OURSELF PERMISSION TO FIND A WAY TO SPEND
MORE TIME AT THOSE ACTIVITIES AND GIVE OURSELF
PERMISSION TO DO SOMETHING A LITTLE LESS
TRADITIONAL. KEEP DOING WHAT YOU LOVE -
NEVER STOP THAT BUT START PAYING ATTENTION TO
WHAT OPPORTUNITIES ARISE THAT YOU COULD HAVE
NEVER EXPECTED IN A MILLION YEARS

*I am Ancient*

THAT COULD BRING YOU THAT MILLION BUCKS. *And in order to bring in the big bucks through certain activities, you need to have the ability to excel at these.*

THE 'PROBLEM' WITH THE 'DO WHAT YOU LOVE AND THE MONEY WILL COME' STATEMENT IS THAT WE EXPECT THE MONEY WILL COME IN ONLY ONE WAY. THE FACT IS, WHEN YOU OPEN UP YOUR CHANNELS OF RECEIVING BY DOING WHAT YOU LOVE - YOU ALSO NEED TO OPEN UP YOUR CHANNELS OF HOW THE MONEY WILL COME. WHEN YOU'RE DOING WHAT YOU LOVE - YOU OPEN THOSE CHANNELS BUT YOU CLOSE OFF HOW FAST THE MONEY WILL COME IF YOU TRY TO CONTROL THE WAY THE UNIVERSE WANTS TO BRING YOU THE CASH. IF YOU KEEP WONDERING WHERE THE MONEY IS AND WHY ISN'T IT COMING, REMEMBER, THAT ALSO CLOSES OFF THE FLOW BECAUSE YOUR FOCUS IS ON THE LACK OF IT BEING THERE.

*What do you think?* WITHOUT HAVING A CONVERSATION WITH YOU WHERE I COULD ASK YOU A GAZILLION QUESTIONS, I THINK YOU ARE SO CLOSE AND HEADING IN THE RIGHT DIRECTION - JUST REMAIN OPEN TO OPPORTUNITIES YOU HADN'T THOUGHT OF BEFORE.

# HOW TO NOT PANIC ABOUT BILLS

Here's a question from my audience...

*Hi Karen,*

*In response to your request for questions, here's my burning question...Is there a difference between attracting things we "want" and things we "need"? I find its easy to feel positive and stay in vibration with the things I want for the future (e.g. bigger house, nicer car) and I know that this works and I have a lot of fun doing it. However when it comes to things I need in the immediate future (e.g. money for bills) I can't help but feel panicked and have difficulty staying in the same vibration. Can you offer me and the other listeners some advice or affirmation to overcome this hurdle? Thanks.*

*One of your many faithful listeners and tips fan,*

*Sally*

Hi Sally - isn't panic the worst!?

This is a great question about whether there is a difference between attracting what we want versus what we need. There is definitely a different vibrational feeling to the words want and need. 'Want' typically implies that we are asking for something we don't currently have and it's something me might expect in the future.  For some people this word also means it's likely something that's a long shot in getting (not expecting it).  How you have used 'want' seems to be used in a way that has a positive vibration for you.

'Need' implies something that one must have that they don't currently have which also implies a bit of desperation.

In any case, I would recommend that any affirmation or visualization for both 'wants' and 'needs' items are made according to the 3P formula.  All affirmations or visualizations should be made:

- in the Present-tense
- as a Personal statement (it's about me or I - not about you, us or we)
- stated in the Positive

For instance, about your bills, you might say something like "All my bills are easily paid on-time and in full."  Then get excited about that!

Years ago I used to regularly feel that panicked feeling when it came to bills.  I would avoid paying them or feel that tightness in my gut when a particularly large bill came in.  What I started to do was put all my bills on automatic payment from my bank account.  What this was telling the Universe was that I was expecting to be able to pay my bills on-time, every month.

Being a vibrational Universe that we live in - it responds and makes it happen easily, on time, in full every month. I rarely ever even think about my bills as it's all taken care of.

I am Exotic

# HOW TO DEAL WITH NEGATIVE MONEY THOUGHTS...

We don't know what we don't know.

The one thing you must come to terms with is that if you don't have money in your life right now there are reasons for that and all those reasons come back to you and choices you have made. OUCH!!!  If the 'ya-but' monster is starting to whirl around in your head with finger pointed at everything and everyone else - know this - if you don't lovingly squash this monster NOW - nothing will change for you.  DOUBLE OUCH!!

Ya - but, the economy.  Ya - but, my job.  Ya - but, my _____(fit in what is appropriate - husband, wife, sister, father, dog...).  Ya - but, the accident.  Ya - but, Ya - but, Ya - but......

The great news is that as soon as you get rid of the finger pointing and blaming and tell the truth - you can start to change your reality.

I want you to do two things for yourself:  Release and Expand.

Release your limiting beliefs, thoughts and feelings about money.  You start this process by saying this declaration as often as you can and I would recommend saying it before you go to sleep "I release NOW all limiting beliefs, thoughts and feelings about money".  You don't actually have to know what those beliefs, thoughts and feelings are (although that can sometimes help and speed up the process) - you just have to put out the intention that you are releasing them.

This allows you to attract more money into your life.

Next, I want you to expand your beliefs about money. Think about the most money you've made in a year and now think about what it would feel like to make that in a month...every month. I can hear the gasps of disbelief from here! I want you to notice if you're having negative feelings or thoughts about this possibility. That's a limiting belief. Yup, so is that one, too (c'mon, the one you just had) :)

The fact is that people who are no smarter, industrious or beautiful than you are earning that kind of money, right now. And, no, they're not all drug dealers! (Did I catch you on that one?)

Start looking for evidence of people earning that kind of money - that will expand your money consciousness. When your money consciousness expands - you increase your ability to attract more.

I am Unconventional

## HOW DO I MANIFEST MORE MONEY?

*Hi Karen,*

*I am having trouble manifesting more money for me. Part of the problem is that I grew up in a family where my mom was always saying that things were too expensive, we don't have enough money, we can't afford it, etc. I have been reading so many different books on the LOA and there are times when I ask for something and right away, I get it. But because I am so hung up on money that deep down, I still feel like I am not deserving of it. I repeat to myself on occasion that I am a money magnet and that money flows to me. And I have started writing in my gratitude journal again. But these thoughts still creep into my head. What can I do?*

*Thanks,*

*Birgit*

———————————

Thanks Birgit for that question!  This is all too common for many, many people.  So many of us were brought up hearing that there isn't enough. And, as you mention, many people don't feel deserving.  You're doing great by starting to repeat the mantra that you're a money magnet and that money flows to me - keep that up and use my Woohoo Method with this to pump up your energy.

184

One of the keys is to turning money issues around is to start paying attention to your language and feelings around money, rich people and free stuff.

Catching yourself in the moment is crucial to learning about what's holding you back. If you ever feel resentful towards people who are spending money 'frivolously' or towards rich people, in general - you're pretty much guaranteeing that you'll never be rich. Rats, hey?

You might be asking what does our attitude towards free stuff have to do with attracting wealth? Well, you'd be surprised. The people that I run across that are always looking for free stuff because they're poor are just ensuring that they'll never have a reason to have to pay for anything. Say what?!

Think of it this way, if you're rich - if you get something for free - it's a great deal, right? Rich people expect to pay for what they want - they are offering something of value (money) for something of value (service or object). Poor people want (or sometimes expect) something for free because they're poor. Does this sound like a mindset that will attract wealth? No, it's a mindset that will attract more reasons to need free stuff.

If we want to attract more money into our life - then we have to WANT to pay for things and be HAPPY to pay full value. If that statement makes your skin crawl and want to run in the other

I am Perfect

direction or if it just makes you angry - BINGO!!! This would be a great time to pay attention because you've just found one of your blocks to wealth.

Hey, I'm not saying that it's not prudent to look for deals - quite the contrary. However, if you're looking for a deal because you can't afford it - guess what you'll attract more of? You're right, the feeling of not being able to afford it. Now, if you can get excited about the future prospect of being able to afford something - you'll be on your way to attracting just that.

**www.theattractioninactionbook.com**

Always adding new resources! Check it out to get your free bonus materials and links to the resources you've read so far in this book

# EXPECTING GREAT THINGS!

Geoff and I are off to the big bright-light city of Las Vegas soon and if you watched my video from last year - you know my 'luck' was not great. Fully accepting my part in creating that, I know when I gamble that I do it for fun and entertainment and I expect to spend money on that activity.

This year I'm working on changing that. How great would it be to come back with a swack o' cash?! Awesome, I'm thinking. In fact, how fun would it be to have so much money that you would have to think about declaring it at the border....!?

If I can cram my video camera into my luggage, I'll take more video when I'm there and let you know how it all panned out.

Expecting great things!

*I am Amused*

187

## COUCH POTATO DREAMS :)

I refuse to hang on to a cold longer than three days. That's all the time I feel I should allot viruses to do their thing.

Right now I have a cold that refuses to play my game, it's outplaying, outwitting and outlasting...sheesh!

The upside is that I've gotten to share this with my husband and we spent the weekend being couch potatoes. Hey, it's January in Canada, what else are we going to do?

There was a particularly large lottery here this past week and so we had fun imagining all the good we would do with $43 million dollars.

What would you do with that much money? Do you ever allow yourself to really feel what it would be like to have way more than enough? If you do allow yourself to really feel this - that is fantastic - keep it going! If you don't, why not? If you're having issues of not having enough money - this would be a great starting point to uncover any blocks.

In the meantime, here's an excerpt from 'God Works Through Faith" by Robert A. Russell.

*"Think in large sums. The more you expect, the more faith will bring you."*

# BILLIONAIRE THINKING

Last month I went to Alexandria Brown's Online Success Blueprint Workshop. I had attended last year but this year was significantly different.

I've watched Ali move her business from a pretty good online business in the past four or five years to now a multi-million dollar business. That has been inspiring!

She introduced us to her coach who is a billionaire. What was amazing about this woman and her rise to her financial status was that it was ALL about her mindset. Which, of course, is what using the Law of Attraction is all about.

Her first job when she moved to London was to work at an exclusive hair salon by Hyde Park. The people that came to see her were very successful people and at her young age of fifteen, she learned that if you want something to happen - you just make it happen. She didn't have any preconceived notions about failure because she wasn't in that environment. Fascinating, huh? It was just simple to her.

Now she owns 22 companies and has 1800 employees and took a business from nothing and in four years sold it for almost a billion dollars. I don't know about you, but to be in the actual presence of someone who just thinks that's easy is kind of mind-blowing. lol

I am Enjoyable

189

Can you, for a moment, go back to a time when you thought ANYTHING was possible? If you can, good - get in touch with that feeling and stay there as much and as often as possible. If you can't - think about someone who might think like that - put yourself in their shoes and get in touch with that feeling. We all have access to this energy any time we want.

One other thing to keep in mind, Ali announced some time ago that she was changing her business. She knew that she wanted to take it to the next level but she didn't know what that was BUT she announced that she was not doing some activities any more. Since then she met her coach, hired her and is now publishing a magazine.

So, next time you are wondering how it's all going to work and you look at some of the most successful people out there and think THEY HAVE IT ALL FIGURED OUT...think again. The 'how's come when you make a decision.

## ACTION - THE DIFFERENCE BETWEEN THINK AND GROW RICH AND THE SECRET

In 1937 a classic was born, Napoleon Hill wrote Think and Grow Rich. Nearly 70 years later a new classic was born in Rhonda Byrne's book and movie, The Secret.

I have to tell you, I'm always amazed when I find another book written so very long ago that gives such straightforward information about how to use what you've already got between your ears to create your life in a far more positive way. Yet, even a hundred years later, it seems to be a 'new' idea and considered to be kind of 'out there' information. Yes, it blows me away that many people don't want to give their mindset the credit for the good fortune they create or conversely, the crap that shows up. I have no clue why this stuff isn't taught in school. Can you imagine how much further ahead in your life you would have been if you lived this information as a kid?

Maybe this is part of the reason, it was pointed out to me recently that the information in The Secret and Think and Grow Rich seem to contradict each other. I guess the confusion can make anyone's head spin out of control and crack up against the reality of their life only to say 'I don't get it so why bother - none of this crap really works anyway'.

It is true though that there is some seemingly contradictory facts between these iconic books. Both talk about the Law of

191

Attraction but the difference between the two has to do with action.  Hill writes that one has to develop a burning desire and then create a detailed plan while Byrne touts that it isn't your job to figure out the 'how'.

Well, you know, both are true to a degree.  I can see how this can be confusing, especially in our action-oriented world where we are all encouraged to do something - anything, as it's better than sitting on your duff.  Right?!  WRONG!

Napoleon Hill wrote of creating a detailed plan AFTER connecting with a burning desire.  The people he studied for this book were all very successful, very rich people of the day.  It's not a surprise that after getting all fired up about an idea that they would want to figure out how it's going to get done, right?

Rhonda Byrne, on the other hand, says that it's not your job to figure out the 'how' and that getting clear about what you want is your main job.  She's consulted with many very successful (and in some cases very rich) motivational speakers of our current day.  There isn't one of those people that contributed to the book and the film that haven't worked to get where they're at today. The difference is how hard they worked or how much action they took.

Because we're an action oriented culture, we expect to be doing something all of the time. The missing piece in both of these books that is alluded to, but not out-right mentioned, is that action IS needed. How often have you been sitting on your couch watching a re-run of Seinfeld and the very thing that you have been dreaming of has dropped in your lap? I haven't heard THAT story once!

The difference is in the type of action that is needed.

INSPIRED ACTION is the only real action to take. You can run around being busy and looking important because you're busy. However, that kind of action will create more stress and fewer results than anyone would wish on their best enemy.

Think about this; remember back to the last time something incredible happened in your life, did you plan every step of the way? I think not. In fact, it is the most incredible events that we attracted in our life because we were in the right place at the right time (hmmm, sounds a little like inspired action might have gotten you to that place?).

This is not to say that many of us haven't experienced incredible events that have been planned out but I wonder how much quicker they would have occurred if we weren't trying to control, plan and manipulate? My guess is that we sometimes get in the way of our own success.

What's the cure? Take a step back and vow to be a human BEING rather than a human DOING. Focus in on what you want and pay attention to the wild and weirdo thoughts that jump into your mind and try acting on those.

# GETTING TO 'KNOW'.....

Do you get frustrated with the whole concept of the Law of Attraction when what you want hasn't been showing up? You're not the only one - every week I get emails from my audience that asks where their stuff is and what do they need to do differently.

How does one keep focus on what they want when it isn't there - I answer that question below....

## WANTS TO LIVE A HIGHER LIFE BUT CAN'T AFFORD THE DRESS

*Hi Karen.*

*I actually don't mind whether this is answered on a podcast or in the newsletter since I get both of them--and they're great. Thank you!*

*I was just listening to The Secret, and I have a question about part of it. Toward the end it's talking about financial success and basically it says it's counterproductive to ask for greater prosperity, then turn around and say you can't afford to buy something because that's the same old non-prosperity mind set that's kept you poor. Well, asking for greater prosperity is wonderful, but it doesn't happen overnight and in between there are things you aren't going to have the money to buy. For*

195

*instance, I may ask "the universe" for a higher paycheck, and see myself earning that money, and be grateful for earning that money, but I'm still not going to be able to buy a new dress right now, and I don't see any way around that. I have to be aware that at this moment I can't go out and buy a new dress. How do I handle this seeming impossible situation--to ask for greater prosperity, yet be aware that at this moment I don't have it so I can't live that higher life style.*

*Claire*

-----

Claire - thanks - this is a great question and quite a conundrum, isn't it? It happens to all of us - we all are wanting something beyond what we have now - it's human nature. The difference in the conscious use of the Law of Attraction is that we want to stay out of the 'feeling' of 'I don't have this' as much as we can. Of course, the more we focus on something not being there, we give that 'lack' our focus and our energy therefore using the Law of Attraction to create more of that lack. None of us want more of what we don't want. However, that's where most of us live just because that's what we've learned.

That's why I like the statement 'absence of evidence doesn't mean evidence of absence'. I first heard this statement as it related to science - I think it may have been a NOVA show I was watching about the universe and galaxies and quantum physics. It is such a great truth when it comes to the Law of Attraction - just because when we are not experiencing what we want in our life right now doesn't mean that it's not coming. It doesn't mean that the energy that you've been putting out there about the greater paycheck or the new dress isn't percolating. And, absence of evidence doesn't mean that it isn't going to show up tomorrow. In fact, so many of us give up our dreams when they are just about to happen.

Our job is to get to that place of KNOWING that what we want is going to show up. Granted, it doesn't always show up in the time frame we would hope but that's usually because of our feelings of 'where is it' is helping to delay what we're waiting for - rats, huh?!

How do you get to the place of KNOWING? Having faith that this process works is one way of getting to that feeling of knowing. Faith can come about in at least two ways - 1. You choose to believe something because others that you trust believe in the concept; 2. You gain faith (and thereby 'knowing') by acknowledging when this process has worked in the past and as it is happening to you in the present. You are acknowledging evidence of this process in your life now. The more you do that - the more you will get to that place of KNOWING. Once you KNOW - it's a done deal.

I would also suggest that you focus on that dress and get excited about it - there are a million ways it could show up for you and be yours. Never worry about the 'how' - the Universe can conspire in a gazillion ways to get that dress to you if you really want it. It's that energy of excitement about the things you want to manifest that brings to you the ways of being able to make it happen.

I'll share a story with you. Geoff, my husband and I appreciate nice cars. At the time of this story (about 10 years ago) - we had been driving Geoff's Mom's old Park Avenue (can you say...boat). It truly was a luxury car in mint condition but not at all what we would consider an appropriate car for us. It just was not a match for our personalities or for who we were becoming.

We decided to sell it (and this is a story in itself) and we washed it, went shopping and came back to the car and there was a note on it asking if we wanted to sell it! We didn't have any signs on it at all indicating that it was for sale.

Okay, that's LOA enough but we sold it and didn't have a car. We needed one and fast. (This is where this story relates to the question) We *expected* to find a great car, we *knew it* - I mean, how does one sell an old boat of a car without advertising if the Universe isn't conspiring to bring us a much better match? As it turns out, Geoff's employer was selling the company BMW 325 that he had been coveting. AND, much to the amazement of a

BMW aficionado friend of ours - we got the deal of the century. (I'll add to this that we sold the car 10 years later for $100 more than what we bought it for AND the buyer was excited to be getting such a great deal! [It was!!])

All in all, get excited about what you want, get to the place of knowing that it's going to happen and stay there until it manifests.

I am Playful

# A PROSPERITY MEDITATION

There is a wonderful woman by the name of Catherine Ponder that has written many books mostly back in the 60's and 70's. I would attribute her writings to be the words that most affected my beliefs around abundance, which has helped me to be living the wonderfully abundant life I live now.

Yesterday I found a meditation by her that I thought I would share with you - I think it is very impactful. This is what it said on the website I found it on....

Catherine Ponder writes from a Christian perspective. Pagans may wish to substitute their own diety form where Ponder mentions God. Those uncomfortable with religion can substitute "The Universe".

*A PROSPERITY MEDITATION FOR GATHERING YOUR MANNA by Catherine Ponder*

*"WHEN I FIND MYSELF IN A FINANCIAL WILDERNESS, IT IS BECAUSE I AM PREPARING FOR A GREATER ABUNDANCE THAN I HAVE EVER KNOWN BEFORE. MY WILDERNESS EXPERIENCE IS MY DIVINE INITIATION INTO THE HIGHER LEVELS OF SUPPLY. I AM BEING FREED FROM ALL FEAR OF LACK. AS I LOOK TO GOD FOR GUIDANCE AND SUPPLY, I AM BECOMING FINANCIALLY INDEPENDENT ON A DAILY BASIS.*

*"I CAN GATHER MY MANNA BY FIRST USING SOMETHING CLOSE AT HAND TO MEET MY NEED. BE IT EVER SO HUMBLE, WHEN I USE WHAT IS CLOSE AT HAND, MY GOOD MULTIPLIES. I CAN BEGIN TO GATHER MY MANNA BY DOING SOMETHING FEARLESS. THE ACT OF BLESSING WHAT IS ON HAND INCREASES IT MIGHTILY. SOMETHING MYSTERIOUS HAPPENS WHEN I BLESS THE SUBSTANCE AT HAND. INSTEAD OF ENVYING ANOTHER'S PROSPERITY, I OPEN THE WAY FOR INCREASED SUPPLY TO COME TO ME.*

*"SINCE WORDS ARE CREATIVE, I CAN GATHER MY MANNA THROUGH SPEAKING FORTH DEFINITE, RICH WORDS OF SUPPLY, EVEN IN THE FACE OF LACK. MY MANNA IS ALWAYS SOMETHING CLOSE AT HAND, AND I ALWAYS HAVE IN MY IMMEDIATE MIDST WHATEVER IS NEEDED TO BEGIN GATHERING MY MANNA. AS I BLESS THE MANNA CLOSE AT HAND AND FEARLESSLY USE IT, IT MULTIPLIES. LORD, I DO GIVE THANKS FOR THE ABUNDANCE THAT IS MINE NOW!"*

I am Festive

I've got this stuck on my wall now, I hope you find it helpful, too. Let's all attract more manna!!!

# HOW DO I GET OUT OF THE PIT OF SURVIVAL-MODE?

*Thank you for offering to answer questions.*

*When life is really difficult, to the survival level and below, how does one get out of the pit? Positive attitude and thinking is very difficult when one hasn't even the time to think.*

*How does this attitude of positive attraction differ from Dan Millman's concepts?*

*Thank you,*

———————————————

Thanks for this question! I wish I could comment on Dan Millman's concepts but I can't - however, YOU have inspired me to look into this - thanks!!

As difficult as it can be to think positively when you are in the midst of survival-mode - it can be done. Victor Frankl who survived through the Nazi death camps lived to write about it in a 'Man's Search for Meaning'. And while I hope you are nowhere near that type of survival-mode - survival-mode is survival-mode no matter where you are.

We do have an estimated 60,000 thoughts a day and your job is to just start having a few conscious positive thoughts. Start with appreciating something - anything! Like the colour of the sky - I find focusing on nature is the easiest way to start the process of appreciation. Start noticing the things you can be grateful for and if you can start your day or end it with writing 1-10 things down that you can appreciate or be grateful for that day - do it! This is extremely powerful and will start the attraction process going the way you want it to.

Let's all send our highest vibrations to this reader - what a powerful gift!

I am Relaxation

# WORK

I am Successful

# AS WITHIN, SO WITHOUT....

Today I was deciding what to write about and when I was driving about I saw this bumper sticker on the car in front of me and it totally epitomizes what I've been thinking and talking about for the past week. The bumper sticker says:

**Business is Great**

**People are Terrific**

**Life is Wonderful**

And, it's riding on the bumper of a Cadillac - an iconic symbol of wealth for many. For whatever reason, bumper stickers tend to tell the truth about people and I have no doubt that this person believes this statement and it shows in his outer world.

This is a truth of the Law of Attraction, what we believe in we see manifested in our outer world. If you had a bumper sticker today and it was telling the truth about your life - what would it say? Next, ask yourself if you would like to change it to a different slogan.

For me, this is one of my new mantras!

# USING THE SECRET TO ATTRACT A JOB

Okay, you've watched 'The Secret', you're all pumped up and feeling great!  AWESOME!

You've got some great information which is providing a launch pad to the rest of your magnificent life!

Now what!?  You follow the principles pretty much as well as you can - but it's a month later and is your dream job anywhere in sight?

Well, KNOW THIS!  If you have been using the information from the movie and following the information from my podcasts and tips letters - your dream job is coming!  I always liked what motivational speaker Brian Tracy said - "what you want - wants you".

It took me a long time to really understand that statement until I got to understand the Law of Attraction.  And here's the explanation - alike things of alike energy come together and so the thought of the thing you want and the thing you want have the same vibration or energy.  The thought and the thing you want have the same energy and they are attracted to each other. So - what you want - wants you.  Easy, hey?  Can't believe how long it took me to get to that - haha - however, I was not well

207

versed in about LOA at all. And that's my excuse, and I'm stickin' to it!

So, the job you want - that pie-in-the-sky dream job - wants you! How awesome of a feeling is that? When you get that and can feel excited about it - you have just increased your vibration and are that much closer.

You see, you're job is to feel good and to remember to find ways to feel good as much as possible. Every moment you are feeling good - the closer you are getting to what you want.

I've walked tons of people through this process and specifically towards finding their dream job and it always comes down to remembering this fact.

Another tidbit - keep focused on the aspects of your dream job that you are after and even when the one you 'THINK' is your dream job comes along and doesn't transpire - have faith! Something even better is coming your way.

Here's a question along the same lines from a reader....

———————————————

## AM I ALLOWING MY DREAM JOB?

*Hello Karen,*

*I have been listening to your podcast and wanted to let you know that it is very helpful. I wrote down the 5 stages/laws of attraction.*

*I interviewed for my dream job a few months ago. The company has stayed in contact with me to let me know they are interested in me, however, as of recently I haven't heard anything.*

*As I listened to your podcast I realized that I am in step 4 – Allow it! I have started to build walls around it because yes I wanted it but with each day my expectations are lowered. So I know I need to get back to allowing it and expecting it and not doubt or ask where the heck is it.*

*I wanted to let you know I really needed this information!*

*Thanks,*

I am Appreciative

---

You are welcome!  Okay, so as I re-read this - looks like it isn't a question after all but I'd like to comment :)

You are in the most difficult part of the attraction process - the Allowing part - stick in there! Your job is to stay focused on the aspects of this job that you are really attracted to AND it's your job to stay feeling good. Don't focus on this particular job - just the aspects you like or love. As I mentioned above - as perfect as it may seem - it may not be as perfect as what is waiting around the corner for you.

Keep your senses tuned to other opportunities or things that just twig your interest - and follow where those lead. You could be very nicely surprised!

Now that I've said all that - it isn't to say that you won't get this job - you certainly could and everything is just waiting for the proper alignment in order for it to be the dream job you've been awaiting!

# THE POWER OF NETWORKING

The opportunities that we want in life come through other people.  Period.

Notice I said 'through' other people - not 'from'.  Everything we desire comes 'from' Source Energy.

So what?   Good question ;)

This past week I've been reminded about the power of connecting with people, introducing myself to people that I'm inspired to connect with - you never know where it's going to lead you.  Actually, we do know.  If you've been really clear in your intentions (Step Two) and taking inspired action (Step Four) - it will lead you to your goal.  The road may be convoluted.  People may come and go in your life but they will all have a hand in moving you to your destination.

Get out there, talk to people - you'll be amazed.

I am Allowing

# SHOULD I WAIT FOR THE JOB I REALLY WANT?

*Hi Karen,*

*I discovered your pod-cast at the beginning of last year after I watched the movie The Secret and starting doing searches on law of attraction. I just want to thank you for what you are doing. You are truly helping many of us out here to stay on track of positivity.*

*I'm a college student in Michigan and will be graduating with my Bachelors in April. In the beginning of last year some cousins and I took a test to get a job working in an automotive plant. We all passed so we were expecting to hear back from the employer around July. Two of my cousins were called back while me and my other cousin were not. At first I was upset and wondered why not us, too, but as I read my bible I came to the conclusion that God was trying to tell me that having the job then would not be best for me.*

*I say this because he knew how important me doing well in those classes were for me and how much time it would require of me to do well on top of the time I would have had to work in the plant. So after that I was satisfied and just did my best in my classes knowing that the job would come. Now I'm in my last semester of school and I feel as though the job is coming, I'm still positive*

212

*about it while at the same time trying to keep my cousin positive about it as well.*

*Here is were I could use your advice. Being a young adult who is responsible for her own education and other bills I understand that I need money, so should I look for another job until the one I really want calls me in or should I wait it out longer without working? For some reason I feel like if I get another job it would mess with the way the law of attraction works and push the job I really want away. Please help me out and tell me how you think I should handle this.*

*Thank You,*

*M*

---

Hi M - I get this question often where people are worried about making a mistake with the law of attraction.

An important thing to remember is that you can't get this stuff wrong. Sometimes what we want doesn't show up in the form we thought it was going to show up in.

It reminds me of the story where a man is in the middle of a flood and so he prays to God (asking - Step Three) asking for God to save him. The story goes that first people in a rowboat came by to help and the man refuses help and says God is going to save him. Then a bigger boat comes by but the man refuses to get in and then a helicopter and again the man refuses.

The man drowns and he gets to heaven and says to God - why did you forsake me? I prayed with all my heart for you to save me! God replies - what did you want? I sent two boats and a helicopter!

We live in an action-based world where the law of attraction is always at work. What usually happens is that we act based out of fear rather than taking inspired action. Know that the Universe has heard your request and it is in the process of delivering it to you - it just might not show up as the exact job you expected. It might show up in a better job! One that matches your exact desires!

The job at the automotive plant didn't work out because it wasn't the right match for you at that point.

Here's what I suggest. Rather than focusing on a specific job - focus on the qualities of the type of job you would really like to have. A job that would make you happy and fulfill whatever other requirements that are important to you. Then act on whatever comes up. Follow your hunches. Be bold. If you hear of a job you want - go get it.

You can use information for anything you desire - not just a job. Focus on the specifics of the bigger picture of what you want rather than the specific thing that has the qualities you want. There's an important distinction there - be specific about the qualities you want in anything you want but refrain from focusing on the specific thing. It may already belong to someone else and therefore you may be putting off your good for longer than you need to!

I am Co-creative

# ATTRACTING BUSINESS

When we're in business, all too often, we fall into the trap of catering to whoever shows up at our doorstep because we are grateful to have ANYONE show up.

When we haven't been specific about whom our ideal customer is – the people that usually show up are not ideal. In fact, often they're cranky, want too much and spend far too little. As business owners and managers, we get tired, disenfranchised and can start to feel bitter. Not a very attractive feeling which doesn't attract the results you want.

One of the first things I have my business clients do is create a list of what the perfect customer would be like. You know, the ones that thrill you when they call and make you feel happy to be in the business you're in and being of service. This can be a compilation of a number of customers but in order to get more of these great customers, you need to be clear about what they're like and how you feel when you do business with them.

Create this list for yourself and get into the feeling state of what it would be like to have all your customers be perfect customers. This activity alone can attract an increase in business and make your job so much more fun.

# HEALTH

I am Clear

217

# DRUG COMMERCIALS AND YOUR SUBCONSCIOUS

There are times in our lives when we are challenged in a one or more areas and it's at these times that we may feel vulnerable to information coming our way.  It's at these times that your main responsibility to yourself is to pay great attention to what is being fed into your subconscious mind.

When we're watching TV, we are in a perfect state for information to be directly input into our subconscious. Advertisers are well aware of this and that's why they spend a great deal of money to advertise on television. This is great if the information is useful and is working for you but more often than not we are being programmed in way that could be detrimental. Now, I'm all for education and marketing however, Geoff and I now make a point of changing channels when the drug company commercials come on.  We're being programmed to think that a heart attack, sexual dysfunction and peeing problems are inevitable….are they really?

If you are honest with yourself, and you're getting to be of a certain age, do you entertain these concerns?  Do some of these commercials make you wonder if you're normal…am I having enough sex?  Wouldn't an erection for more than ½ an hour be a concern never mind FOUR HOURS!!!  Is that heart flutter I'm having a result of too much caffeine or MSG or am I having a heart attack?

218

YIKES!! These thoughts are not healthy and what do you think they attract? There are some that believe that the dramatic increase in some health issues is a direct result of focus on these disease processes. True? I don't know…all I can tell you is that it's far better for you to focus on how great you feel rather than what could be wrong.

By all means, educate yourself to understand important signs of health issues but don't make that your main focus.

I am Pleasure

# BIGGER?

**NOTE TO READERS ABOUT THIS QUESTION: I really deliberated with myself as to whether I add this question in its entirety to this book.  I came to the conclusion that there are probably a number of readers who might have the same type of question and so I am treating this as a serious enquiry.  This reader took the time to email me and I appreciate that effort.  I changed the word in brackets so your spam-filter would allow this email through when I sent this out as part of my ezine. **

*"Hello. I have a question. I'm just wondering if the Law of Attraction work on genetics on your physical body. If I were to visualize myself with a bigger (member) would it work on this? Or if I were to visualize myself more muscular? "*

---

Yes.

Haha - Okay, I would love to just leave it at that but I said I would treat this question seriously.  We know that the body has amazing, responsive qualities to it.  We know that, for example, people with multiple personalities can exhibit a very serious disease process while in one personality and yet while in another personality the disease ceases to leave any trace of evidence.

Visualizing (fantasizing - as I talked about in my last tips letter) your body to look/be different has a powerful, transformative ability. We all do it all the time. Body-builders imagine a specific muscle looking a certain way and through that visualization and action - it happens. Thin people imagine themselves fat and they make it so over time. I think the body may have some limitations - but who am I? Science and anecdotal evidence tells us otherwise daily.

The real question that came to mind for me when I read this question is "what is the real feeling you're after?" And for those of you who are guffawing - stop it - I AM serious. Essentially, when we want something, anything in life, it's because we want to feel a certain way. Whether it be powerful, secure, loved, happy - you name a positive feeling - there's something we want that will give it to us. So, if you want a body part to be different - my question to you is that - what feeling will changing that body part give you. It's not the change in the body part you want - it is the feeling it will give you. That's what you want to focus on.

*I am Fantastic*

## CAN YOU ATTRACT BEING HEALTHY?

There were studies done years ago that have been quoted over and over where bodily fluids (either saliva or tears) had been tested when people were in different emotional states. What was found was people who were in strong negative emotional states released a variety of chemicals into their body that were actually quite lethal.

Modern science recommends lots of sleep and ways to release stress. What keeps us up at night and creates stress in our lives? Our thoughts about events, people and things and the meaning we give them gets us and keeps us in these states. Remember nothing has meaning except the meaning we give it.

Law of Attraction starts with our thoughts and feelings. If our thoughts can produce states of emotion and biological changes in our body it stands to reason that we have far more control in attracting health. Of course, eating right and exercising is a major key but if you don't manage your thoughts - you'll end up being a victim of them.

All too often, you see people who do everything right - they manage their weight, eat right and exercise yet they keel over and die anyways. What's up with that? Doesn't seem to leave much hope for those of us that don't do everything right. Not so, look at Winston Churchill - he lived into his 90's, was very overweight and he smoked and drank daily and lived through some pretty stressful times. Now I don't recommend that but it just shows you that something else was at play with him and there are plenty of others around us that also thrive.

I think it would be interesting to see what the main motivation of the person who was doing everything right - what did they focus on - what were their most dominant thoughts around their health? I suspect many people may be conditioned to do these great things for their body in order to avoid something like a disease or illness rather than doing it to be something, or move towards something such as being health or fit. It all comes back to whether you're living in a mindset of lack (I don't want to die or get sick) as opposed to one of abundance (I am healthy, I feel great).

Here's a few things I would recommend:

- When you find yourself focusing on illness or disease - shift your thoughts to focus on your well-being. (ie - rather than thinking I better eat these greens to avoid getting cancer - instead think I think these greens will make me feel great and I like the taste of them) This is a slight shift but you can see the difference in focus - 'cancer' vs. 'feel great'.
- Do what makes you feel good. When you are feeling good, you'll attract what you want and what you're

focusing on.  This is an upward spiral that gets better and better.

- If you aren't feeling healthy right now, do something to distract you that will make you feel good like watching a funny show or listening to something inspirational. When you do this, you allow your natural well-being to show up when your focus is elsewhere.

# THE POWER OF BEING CENTERED

How in touch with your body are you? When your mind is relaxed is your body relaxed, too? If someone was to touch your shoulder and neck muscles right now would they be loose or could would you need a jackhammer to soften them up?

Are you aware of where you carry your negative emotions? Do you actively release your negative thoughts and feelings daily? Are you able to make decisions quickly and decisively?

What I've found for many people, and I'm as guilty as anyone at times, is that they're walking around as tightly wound balls of unexpressed negative energy. Many believe that this lack of ease in our body and our life is what causes disease or dis-ease.

When negative energy is not released it attracts more negative energy or more things to feel negatively about and this is never good for your overall health.

What do you do about this? Find ways to release these feelings by taking on some new activities – these will help you to get centered. Here's what I recommend:

- Exercise – even additional walking can help
- Meditation – start with 5 to 6 minutes of quieting your mind – this will allow you to get in touch with your spirit. You already know how to do this....think of the

225

moments you're zoning out. I remember this so strongly as a kid where I would zone out and start to feel my body floating but firmly linked to my consciousness in my head.

- Do the Sedona Method.
- Connect with Nature – get out and spend some time outdoors and do this alone to give your mind some time to connect with this powerful energy.
- Have your own Conversation with God (or the Universe, Spirit..whatever name works for you), Neale Donald Walsch is not the only one that has this ability. We all do. I recently started this practice by writing a question out and then waiting for an answer. Writing long hand gives the space for me for the answer to come and usually before I finish writing – I already have a response.

Try these things and I expect you'll start to feel more centered and feel more able to take on anything!

# POWER OF SUGGESTION

Years ago I became aware of the impact my thoughts and words had on my health. When I was working at my job and needed a holiday or even just a day off, I would invariably have this thought, 'I feel tired, I must be coming down with something' and guess what would happen? Yes, I'd get a cold and I'd stay home for a day ( I would feel too guilty to stay home for longer than that) and the cold would hang around for a couple of days.

Then one day it dawned on me that I really was just tired and needed a day off and didn't need to create a cold. From that day on, I rarely get colds that require time off but I now pay better attention to when I'm tired and I make sure I get the rest and time off that I need.

How does this work for you in your life? Do you worry about getting sick or hurt? Is there an illness that affected family members that lingers in the back of your mind as something to worry about? Do you have people in your life that talk about illness or don't do this or that because you'll get sick? Turn that energy off now!

I know people have the best intentions with their warnings (about wearing sunscreen, not smoking, etc.) but it's the focus of their energy that concerns me. When someone we care about warns us very loudly that we're going to get skin cancer if we don't put sunscreen on – what do you think that's attracting?

227

What is your subconscious hearing and focusing on?  Sunscreen or cancer?  Which has more emotional impact?  I can guarantee that the focus immediately goes to cancer which has a visceral and negative energy to it.

What we focus on with theeling – we attract.  Don't do this to yourself and don't do it to others.  There are other ways of communicating concern in a way that doesn't scare the bejesus out of the people you care about.

That's why I don't support any cause that is touted as a "War against…" or a "Fight against…".  Talk to me about possibility, talk to me about finding a cure – I'm all over that!

Also, if you find yourself in a position where you really are facing difficult health issues and you feel it's not your time to check out yet – do everything in your power to surround yourself with people who only speak positively including your health professionals.  Talk in possibility not medical statistical probability.  I don't think there is a health issue on the face of this planet (or at least very few) that someone hasn't recovered from – seek that information out and get inspired.  Taking these steps could make life and death difference.

# TRANSITION

If you've come this far in your search to understand the Law of Attraction and you've decided to entertain that everything is made up of energy then you also know that energy never dies, it just changes form.

Recently I read one of Wayne Dyer's older books '*You'll See It When You Believe It*' where he talks about different states of consciousness and likens our dream life, our conscious life and our larger spirit life as states of transition. He also makes a case for the possibility that life after death is just an awakening similar to our awakening after a dream. I like that thought – it makes the process that much less scary to me. I can live with that – lol! Like I have a choice, however, it does make me feel safer and less afraid.

Another explanation I heard awhile ago from an Abraham-Hicks recording was their explanation of Alzheimer's. Essentially, they were indicating that these souls were just taking their time to release themselves from their life. They weren't enjoying themselves anymore and so the process of forgetting was preferable than living the way they were. They hadn't decided to 'check out' yet because they had loved ones wanting to hold on to them. I don't know if we'll ever know for sure whether or not this is true but this is comforting to me as well.

I am Classy

When my father got sick a number of years ago, he had already had Parkinson's for a number of years and he was tired and very frustrated at this lack of ability to do the things he liked to do. It looked for a bit like he was going to recover and then he had a set back where it was clear he was going to be even worse off – a reality he would have hated living.

His time to transition was around my birthday and I know there were many who were silently praying that 'my day' wouldn't be his last. I believe he hung on for an extra two days for that reason. Honestly, his ability to let go was a strong blessing and lesson for me in my own journey to understand this life and if he had left on my birthday, I would have been honored with that gift.

Now I know some may be appalled at that statement and some will totally get it – it all depends on how you feel about life as an on-going, non-dying energy.

I always advocate for looking for explanations that make us feel better about the inexplicable. After all, no one really does know the reality so let's focus on what makes us feel good about the process that also allows us to live a fuller life in the now.

# SUCCESS STORIES

*I am Splendid*

# A SUCCESS STORY ABOUT WORTHINESS...

*I have recently realized that I have been living by the law of attraction my entire life and never understood it. I have controlled everything with my mind without realizing how much I influenced things that seem completely out of my control. If I interviewed for a job and spent time to think about how much I was going to wow the interviewer, I'd always get the job. If I focused on getting something I really wanted, it came to me. When money was tight for us, I would have days where I felt the newspaper classified ads spoke to me and on those days a much needed item would be in the ads for sale at a price we could afford.*

*As I look back on how things have worked out for me, I usually start out filled with positive thoughts and things work out my way. When I was upbeat and positive, everything in life fell in place. Money, great job, love, and friendship it all came to me. When I allowed myself to get down and negative, everything went wrong. I got into an abusive relationship, the great jobs turned awful, unexpected bills arrived and friends were lost for no real reason.*

*This cycle has gone on for my entire life. I realize I have never felt completely worthy of the gifts I have been given. Instead of enjoying the gifts and visualizing more to come to me, I start to*

*feel guilty and things start to crumble before my eyes. I would
start to think I had sweet talked my way into a job I didn't
deserve, maybe a better candidate had lost out because I put on
a false front. My relationships would suddenly start to feel
different; I would convince myself I was not as good as the
people around me and feel like they knew it. It wouldn't be long
before that became a reality. My dream car suddenly turned into
a lemon. I could go on and on....*

*I now know that I must focus on enjoying the gifts. If I was
worthy enough to attract them, I am worthy enough to keep
them. This is my new focus.*

*My new mantra:*

**I was a good enough person to attract it, therefore I deserve it.
- and more**

*Elaine*

I am Luxury

---

Thanks Elaine for sending in your story - this is such a great
example of how the Law of Attraction works!

A virus of 'not good enough' exists in our society and is so
insidious it is absolutely shocking. People who you would never

think suffered from a lack of self-worth do suffer. It's an absolute tragedy.

Can you imagine how fantastic things would be if we all felt worthy and secure? For starters, there would be no gangs, likely no violence, no need for drugs and the list could go on and on.

And it all begins and ends with our thoughts. The key is to keeping our focus on the positive 'stuff'. Enlist a friend to help you keep your focus. Heck, enlist a few friends to do this and ensure they are on the same wavelength as you and want to attract nothing but good into each other's lives.

# IN THE RIGHT PLACE AT THE RIGHT TIME

I want to share an experience with you. I was on my way home from work when the Subway was shut-down due to a problem at one of the Stations. After trying unsuccessfully to get a cab home I went back to the subway station.

There, also trying to figure out what to do was a friend from work. I had been trying to decide whether or not to talk to her in her professional capacity all day.

She needed a cell phone to call her husband to give her a ride, I had one.

We were able to help each other out and I got the conversation I needed with her plus a ride home. To make matters even more interesting, she and her husband were on their way out for dinner and I had the phone number to the restaurant they were late for on my cell phone so they were able to call. They are both very happy positive people. They use the Law of Attraction without even knowing what it is. It came through for all of us.

I am Spicy

235

## STOPPED TRYING SO HARD

It took me quite awhile to realize just how simple life can be when we relax and stop trying so hard then everything falls into place. I've learned from your tips to believe and visualize things coming my way.

What I realized is when I am relaxed and not worried, I can see opportunity more clearly and people navigate towards me in a positive way. Everything happens for a reason and what we resist persists. I've learned to make peace with the moment and even when you don't like the way some things are going, afterwards you see that it was always perfect.

Jo-Ann Mangione
www.wellnessmoms.com

# SUN WORSHIPPER HEALS SELF

I believe as human beings we have such incredible power to change the direction and course of our lives if we believe we can.

I have believed in The Law of Attraction for many years of my life and truly know it has had a key role in allowing me an incredible life journey thus far and will serve me well into the future.

This story about The Law of Attraction and healing happened to me about ten years ago. I always have been and always will be a sun worshipper, you may call me crazy if you wish, but I don't believe in sun screen and has always enjoyed the benefits of natural sunshine and the outdoors.

It had been a fairly hot summer that particular year and there was a lot of talk in the media in this part of West Coast Canada that skin cancer cases will surely be on the rise and people should be aware to stay out of the sun or protect yourself.

I generally would have paid no attention to this kind of media talk; however we were being constantly bombarded with it to a point where it made me feel it was wrong to be outside doing yard work in a tank top.

*I am Positive*

237

As the summer was going by I began to notice a round shaped spot developing on my upper left arm, at first I gave it no real thought that it was anything more than a freckle or mole. As more time had passed the shape was taking on a defined look, it resembled one of the images I remembered seeing on one of the news programs when they were taking about skin cancer. I did some further research and came to the conclusion I very well could have a problem on my hands.

Let's just say this did not sit well with me. I had loved the natural sunshine for thirty plus years and was not ready to end my relationship with it.

In a calm state I focused on my options, and what would work best for me, visualizing the outcome I wished. Going to a doctor was not an option for me at that point, I did not want to be told to stay out of the sun and be treated with textbook medicine and advice.

I decided I would heal myself using the principles of The Law of Attraction. My vision and take on my situation was very clear to me. I could not and would not believe sunshine; something I had loved for so long would want to cause me illness. I also came to the conclusion all the fear and news hype about the so called evils of being in the sun had probably had some sort of effect on my subconscious.

From that day on, two to three times a day I would place my right hand over my left arm where the mole had developed. I would send healing energy to the area focusing on the elimination of the mole and attracting a healthy looking arm that would love sunlight.

I never once gave into the concept this could not be healed, I continually attracted positive energy to the affected area. Within three to five days I was sure I was seeing quite a difference in the area. I started to expose my arms to the sun again and it felt great. After one full week there was a huge difference the mole shape had shrunk and changed color dramatically. Within the month there was nothing left but a faint outline of what was.

The mole has never come back and I still enjoy full on sunshine to this day-sunscreen-less.

Peace

Geoff

I am Powerful

# APPLYING STEP FIVE

Dear Karen,

This morning I was reading a book recommended by you in one of your e-mails. It's by Ester and Jerry Hicks (The Teachings of Abraham) and is called ASK AND IT IS GIVEN. In this book there are 22 processes that can help you get rid of the resistance and allow the Source Energy to flow through you more easily. So I read the first process which is called 'The Euphoria of Gratitude' and it teaches us to give thanks every time we can: while we are waiting in a queue, when we feel happy and want to feel even happier or just any time we can afford to do this - appreciate the things that make us feel happy (or even the ones that don't). So it said "Have a look around you and find an object to appreciate. Then think about it for a while, how beautiful it is, how useful it is... how it makes you feel happy and enjoy your life (this is not exactly what the book says! I'm paraphrasing it). Then after you do this find another thing to appreciate and then another one and so on until in a few days you realize you do it automatically"

So I was in my room and the first thing I started appreciating was my computer: how great it was that I had it, I can talk to my friends and keep in touch with them on Facebook, the e-mails I get from you and everything.. Then I saw a picture of my friends (who are now away from me) and me and I started thinking about them and I felt great about it. (allow me to tell you that here in Bulgaria every year on March 1st we put ourselves special bracelets and we should take them off when we see a swallow (the bird), but **never** before that! but last night my bracelet teared in two pieces and I thought: "oh my God, that is not doing any good at all!" So I left it and went to sleep.) but this morning because I had started appreciating my life, because I had started celebrating my life I went to the living room and what I saw was my bracelet fixed!!! Can you believe this?? Someone (I think it was my mom or my dad) had fixed it!!!! Something I thought was never going to happen happened and I think it is because of that process of giving thanks I was practicing earlier today. Because I know from you (step 5) that as soon as you start appreciating things in life the Universe will give you more things to be grateful for!! So this is what it actually did! It brought me more things to be grateful for! and this is so important for me. Im only 16 and Im not seeking for attracting more money now or anything, I just want to improve the happiness in my life!!!!!

I have been applying Step 5 in my life and I think it is one of the most important things people should do even if they haven't got what they want yet :) (Actually I don't think there is a person that has all they want because we always want more! And that's great!!)

So the point if my e-mail is that we should celebrate the little things that happen to us plus I think it is a very good example for beginners - people who have just started learning of the Secrets of Prosperity.

Karen, THANK YOU very very much for reading my e-mail. the fact you've given it your attention is very important to me. As ive told you before - it makes me feel great when I send you an e-mail or every time I contact you and share a bit of my experience with such an inspirational person like you!

~THANK YOU~

Have a Great Day,
Tsvety Mavrodieva
xx

# THE PERFECT RING

Hi Karen,

A couple of months ago, my boyfriend of 3 years and I decided that we wanted to get married. He was out of a job at the moment and being a gentleman he didn't want to propose without a ring that I could cherish forever.

Every night before bed I would close my eyes and just visualize the perfect ring on my finger. I didn't have an image of what it looked like but I knew so strongly that whatever I got would be perfect that I could feel the ring sitting on my finger!! Night after night this was a ritual.

One day we were at the mall and happened to stop into a jewelry store and started talking to the sales clerk. She showed us this beautiful ring that I totally fell in love with and it turned out to be very inexpensive. I was so excited and told my boyfriend that with a few changes (I wanted the center stone to be a sapphire instead of a diamond) that it would be my perfect ring.

I now had an image to work with, and every single night I would feel the ring on my finger before I went to bed.
2 weeks later he proposed and my ring was the most perfect thing in the world (next to my boyfriend) and it turned out that

he had some savings stashed away that was exactly the amount that the ring ended up costing!!

We are now in full swing of wedding planning and are soo excited to start our marriage!!

Marta Gerech

# DEPOSIT FOR $10,000

Karen,

Thanks for your tips. They keep me thinking positive.

I want to share my success story with you. I've been intentionally using law of attraction since about Sept 2007. I'm no master, but I have had some interesting things materialize for me since then. The clearest example stems from one of the 22 processes (abraham/hicks) - I wrote out a deposit slip in my checkbook for $10,000. I sat it on top of my check book on my desk. I saw it all the time and I just kept saying to myself " I've got to deposit that 10,000." or I'd see it and feel safe and secure that I had that money.

Time passed and I kept looking at that deposit slip and knew it was coming. Then one day while I was on the phone with my Mom she mentioned that a young couple had offered them a large sum of money for her childhood home, my folk had fixed up as a rental. They were going to give me $5000. Cool, right. Time passes I'm still looking at that deposit slip (patiently). I'm on the phone with Mom again a few months later and she informs me that the little family farm of which I'm an shareholder will now start paying me $2500 quarterly. Voila! Interestingly it took me awhile to make the connection but eventually I got it, and the strength of my intentions has delivered this $10,000 annually. I still have the old deposit slip, but I've got a new one, one top for $25,000.  I'll get back to you on that.

Carolyn E.

# DOUBLED HIS TAX REFUND

I wanted to thank you first of all for having such an amazing impact in so many people by using your gift, your secret, the law of attraction .

My name is Kevianno and I came across your Podcast on ITunes and downloaded as many as I could. I listen to your Podcast morning and night; I'm truly a believer of the law of attraction.

Every year when tax season comes, I usually receive about the same amount of money, this year I visualized, felt, embodied, and believed more money coming. It manifested and came true. I received Double the amount and it came even quicker than usual .

The Law of Attraction is reality.

Kevianno

## VISUALIZED AND GOT HER DREAM JOB

Dear Karen,

I've been following your podcasts for the past year. Throughout last year I had been very unsatisfied with the direction of my career & was very undecided about what to do, if I should continue in my current field or try something new. Well, I began by visualizing what my dream job would be like, what my office would look like, what my co-workers would be like, even down to the colored paperclips! A month ago, a former classmate of mine contacted me about a job opening in her department. I applied, sailed through the interview, & signed for it last week. I start next month & am so excited! I am proof that this law of attraction thing works! My new visualization goal is to get in shape! I'm visualizing myself running a marathon. I'll send you a picture when I finish it!

Amanda Nguyen

# SCHOLARSHIP TO FINISH DOCTOR'S DEGREE

I'm a 27 year old student and I'm working on my doctoral thesis. I earn my money by giving communication and presentation courses. Last year was a very hard one, because I had no jobs and so I couldn't earn any money. During summer the situation became worse – I had bills to pay, but all my savings were eaten up.

The professor, who parents my thesis, asked me, if I want to apply for a scholarship. I said "yes" in a second, because I knew this would be my financial rescue. So I wrote the application and visualized that all would end well. But "real life" didn't stop knocking on my door. I lived in a situation in which I really had no money at all and tried to imagine that I have more than enough of it.

So – unhappiness and negative thoughts came back to me, until I felt trapped and paralyzed and had no hope inside me. I couldn't even think that there would ever be a change. I even thought hard about quitting my work on my thesis and find myself a "proper" job. I tried to push my thoughts back to the good stuff, but it was very hard and the bad ones always came back to me.

*I am valuable*

So, finally, at the end of the summer, I got a letter from the bureau which gives the scholarships – and, you will know by now, they told me, that my application was declined. I felt very desperate, but there was also a little voice inside me that said: I know that this would happen. I mourned for 3 days. On the third day I started to make a plan. I wrote down the things I didn't want in my life anymore: no money, no work, … and then the things I want to have in my life: my doctors degree, a job I could earn my living with,… And I knew that these things are more important than the things I didn't want. I felt my inner strength again, I was confident that I would achieve my doctor's degree – even without a scholarship.

So I started to search for new jobs and wrote on my thesis. Within 2 or 3 days I felt totally new. I was terminated to achieve my goal, and I was motivated to do what I have to do for it.

One week after the letter with the decline, my cell phone rang at 7 o'clock in the morning. I wondered who would call me in the middle of the night – it was the scholarship bureau. The woman on the phone told me, that somebody had rejected his scholarship and that I would be the next on the list to receive one.

I couldn't believe what she told me. And I couldn't believe what I had *done* within 7 days. I changed the world through a change in my feelings, my thoughts and my inner attitude. This was the moment, where I completely *understood* my power.

Today I'm really fine. I even get more jobs than before – although I don't need them anymore because of the scholarship. But some of them I accept – just because it's fun to do some courses. Now I live the life I visualized last summer – thanks to the universe.

Claudia Langosch

I am unlimited

# MANIFESTED TICKET TO SEE GORE VIDAL

This is not my only success story using the Law Of Attraction tools you teach, however, it's the most fun!

A couple of years ago, I was at the UCLA Festival of Books in Los Angeles - and my one goal was to hear my favorite author, Gore Vidal, speaking. We got trapped in freeway traffic on the way and the festival was hot and crowded - and the venue where Mr. Vidal was scheduled to speak was all the way on the other side of the campus - and by the time I got where I wanted to be - I was cranky and miserable.

THEN, I FOUND OUT, I NEEDED A TICKET TO GET IN!!! I didn't know that... But, determined as I was - I got into the line for the people without tickets - along with approximately 500 other cranky folks. From where I stood, it was certain all the available seats in the venue would be filled by the time I got to the door. I stewed and grumbled and bemoaned my sad state....

Then, I remembered what it was that I WANTED! I wanted to see Gore Vidal! So, I got very excited about that prospect. I smiled! I pictured me! Inside! With Gore! I got all tingly about it from head to foot.

A few minutes later, the line of ticket holders began to file past my line, on their way into the venue. A woman - a complete stranger - stopped next to me, and said (I kid you not) "I have an extra ticket, would you like it?" !!!!

I saw Gore Vidal!

Thanks Karen!
Lisa Pedersen

I am Graceful

## RECOVERING ADDICT USES LOA

Karen, I don't have a specific question right now, just comments.

I am a recovering addict and have almost 6 years clean. I was homeless and completely hopeless. I used heroin, meth, cocaine, alcohol, pot, LSD and other drugs for 18 years. I found Narcotics Anonymous and got clean.

My life has completely turned around but I always have felt like something was missing until I watched The Secret 2 months ago. Then I found your podcast and a couple others and have been actively applying this stuff in my personal and professional life. Every area of my life is better and I'm living with deeper gratitude every day.

The woman who I have had a secret crush on for 4 years was on my list, until I heard you suggest putting the qualities that person has that I find attractive on my want list (or my "already have" list) instead of the actual person. Plus three weeks ago she barely even knew who I was. So I asked for someone with these qualities and gave it lots of attention and emotion. I had not seen her around in months. About a week after making my list she showed up at my job and told me she needed to discuss a mutual client of ours. We had a nice talk and I went about my business.

Later I found out she told a co-worker of mine that she thought I was funny and interesting...or something. Anyway, I asked her out and we went for coffee and it was fun, but not earth shattering by any means. I thought she kinda gave me the brush off but she just called me today asking if I wanted to do something soon. I'm blown away and know that this stuff is working.

Thank you for how you present this info in a useful manner. Looking forward to more Podcasts and further success as I get better at using the Law Of Attraction!!

R.

---

Thank you so much for sharing your great success story!

I think it's a great tribute to the fact that one can rebound from any lousy situation they find themselves in. To be hooked on those drugs and come out the other side to move closer to the things you want in life is also a true testament to the human spirit and the power of focus, desire and action!

For all of you out there who are feeling that you're in a tough spot - take heart! It CAN be done no matter what your starting point is!

I am vibrant

Thanks also for bringing attention to my suggestion about focusing on the qualities that you want in a person rather than the specific person. It's a great reminder that all any of us is looking for when we decide that we want something is to feel a certain way. That's all we want - is to feel an emotion - any emotion - whether it's exhilaration, love, joy, spontaneity, excitement or purpose.

Your job, when working with the Law of Attraction, is to look 'behind' the object of your desire and find the essence of what it is you want to feel. When you can get in touch with that - bingo, bango, bongo - you are in vibrational harmony and what you desire will be knocking on your door.

# DO YOU EXPECT SUCCESS?

Expectation in receiving what you ask for is one of the main keys to the Law of Attraction. By having that vibration of expectation - you're telling the Universe that you KNOW it's coming. This automatically puts you in vibrational harmony with the thing you want to attract.

Today I'm going to share with you one of the many fabulous success stories I receive on an on-going basis. This is a story of how the law of attraction can be used for business. This is such a great story because the writer is looking for what he wants and guess what?! He finds it!

**THE LOA HIGHWAY TO SUCCESS.....**

Karen,

Thanks for the opportunity to share this story.

Several months after watching The Secret, our family went on our yearly vacation to Northern California. We own a custom label water bottle business and recently had our truck vinyl wrapped to advertise the company. We usually would not drive this vehicle on vacation but decided to put the Law of Attraction to the test. My intention was to obtain new customers located in California (we are based out of Phoenix, AZ).

257

The entire trip I constantly looked around trying to catch people noticing the truck and taking down our company information. Needless to say, every person I saw seemed to be writing the information down or on the phone calling someone to pass along our information. I really got to the point where everywhere I looked, people seemed to be looking at our vehicle. With the truck being wrapped that is entirely possible but it was more fun believing they were all interested in our company. I don't know that I've ever been so excited about something that would seem trivial, but it was lots of fun and I "KNEW" we were going to get calls.

So, there we were on a San Francisco, CA freeway traveling five miles per hour in complete traffic congestion traveling towards the toll booth to cross the San Francisco Bay Bridge. Once again I looked over at the car next to us (a nice black sports car) and sure enough the guy was looking over checking out the company truck. Not more than a few seconds later I hear a car horn going off from the same location as the black sports car. I look over to find the guy in the car leaning out his window waving his business card asking us to contact him. It must have been quite a sight to watch both of us leaning out of our vehicle windows while still driving down the freeway trying to drive close enough to exchange business cards. Although neither of us will become Hollywood stunt car driver we managed to exchange business cards and have a brief conversation. You could imagine my pure excitement by this experience and immediately recognized the

Law of Attraction at work. That experience was fantastic and really set the stage for a great relaxing and peaceful vacation for the entire family.

The story doesn't end there, within weeks of that meeting the company this person represented became one of our largest customers (at 173 stores located through-out the United States).

Life is perfect!!!

Danny Clark

www.waterpromo.com

_____

Thank you Danny for taking the time to share this story - it's fantastic.

The Law of Attraction is present and active in all parts of our lives not just our personal life. When using this Law actively, simply amazing things can happen in your professional life too! I hear almost everyday how business owners, sales people and front line service people (just to name a few) use the Law of Attraction to increase their business, their bottom line AND provide great service to their customers. It's a win-win situation. Or, like Michael says in the TV comedy series The

Office (for those of you who watch this hilarious show) - it's a win-win-win situation.  You win, the customer wins and ultimately everyone wins when people get what they want because that feeling, that vibe spreads contagiously.

Thanks again for this success story,

## CREATING A BIGGER LIFE CANVAS

I've been utilizing principals of LOA since 2002. I've been feeling like the more I use it, the more questions come up about how it works in specific situations going on in my life. LOA is very powerful and sometimes I create things and then want ways to manage my "creations" in the best way. Other times, I just want to use LOA more purposefully and intentionally.

I went looking for a mentor and found Karen via her website. Her experience in LOA, and our regular coaching sessions, have helped me navigate several big chapters in my life this year in the areas of love and relationships, new creative projects, a new job environment and exciting new career success. Karen's ability to support and challenge me are key to my creating on a much bigger "life canvas" than I used to. I look forward to the insights and aha moments that come out of my sessions with Karen!

DW

# HOW TO REACH US

**No Matter Where You Are, Karen Luniw Can Help You Attract What You Want!**

If you would like more information about how Karen Luniw or her team can help you or your organization, please visit www.KarenLuniwInternational.com

There you will find information on:

- Five Steps To Attract Anything You Want System(s)
- The Business Attraction System
- Coaching Programs
- Workshops and Teleseminars

You can speed up your progress and break down your blocks to what you want quicker by working with Karen directly or with one of her programs listed above.

To connect with Karen and her team today, please just drop an email to info@karenluniwinternational.com and someone will get back to you shortly.

Karen speaks to groups throughout the world both in-person or by teleconference. If you would like Karen to speak at your event or to your group – please contact us for availability by emailing info@karenluniwinternational.com.

## ABOUT KAREN LUNIW

Personal and Business Attraction Expert, Karen Luniw is the creator of the very popular ITunes podcast *"The Law of Attraction Tips"*. This podcast has been downloaded over 1.5 million times by people all over the world. Women with personal and business mindset challenges come to Karen to attract more from life and business, using tools from her *"Five Step* and *Business Attraction Systems."* Her clients are smart, driven women throughout Canada and the US that range from Moms to Entrepreneurs.

Karen has a very real, down-to-earth approach and each client clearly experiences that Karen practices what she teaches. She can confirm that the Law of Attraction has worked for her and it can absolutely work for you. Karen's clients learn to use a new mindset and other powerful tools to get anything they desire through her coaching and products.

She's also created a Podcaster Blueprint so any business person can create a podcast to attract more clients.

Karen lives in the beautiful Okanagan Valley with her husband Geoff and two min-pins, Chili and Pepper.

You can learn more about the products, services and this book's bonuses at www.theattractioninactionbook.com and sign up for Karen's free newsletters that are jam-packed with timely tips you can use.

LaVergne, TN USA
02 November 2010
203107LV00005B/15/P